DISCARD

Mystery of the

DARK MAGIC

Mystery of the DARK MAGIC

marvelkids.com

Printed in the United States of America. First Paperback Edition, November 2016 10 9 8 7 6 5 4 3 2 1 Library of Congress Control Number: 2016932823
FAC-029261-16260   ISBN 978-1-4847-3127-7

Cover illustrations by Ron Lim and Andy Troy
Designed by Kurt Hartman

SUSTAINABLE
FORESTRY
INITIATIVE
Certified Sourcing
www.sfiprogram.org
SFI-01415

Starring
DOCTOR
STRANGE

By **BRANDON T. SNIDER**

Illustrated by
KHOI PHAM, SIMONE BOUNFANTINO,
and CHRIS SOTOMAYOR

Los Angeles
New York

FEATURING YOUR FAVORITES!

DOCTOR STRANGE

WONG

THE ANCIENT ONE

BROTHER VOODOO

SCARLET WITCH

IRON FIST

WHITE TIGER

THOR

LOKI

IRON MAN

CAPTAIN
MARVEL

FALCON

NIGHTMARE

EYE OF
AGAMOTTO

WAND OF
WATOOMB

CLOAK OF
LEVITATION

The Story of DOCTOR STRANGE

As a young man, **Stephen Strange** always believed in himself first and foremost. After graduating medical school with honors, Strange became one of the most gifted surgeons in the world. His practice thrived, garnering him wealth and attention. It also brought out his selfishness and arrogance.

As a doctor, Strange was known for his skill and precision, but in his personal life, he was reckless and irresponsible. One evening he took his favorite car out for a spin, only to lose control and crash it into a tree. His colleagues saved his life, but Strange's hands were damaged beyond repair. His amazing gifts were lost, and he would never be able to perform surgery again.

Instead of allowing anger and frustration to consume him, Strange went on a spiritual journey to the mountains of Tibet, where he encountered the **Ancient One**, a being with vast magical powers. The Ancient One taught Strange humility and caution, training him in a new discipline—the mystic arts.

When the time came, the Ancient One passed on to a new plane of existence and bestowed on Stephen Strange the mantle of **Sorcerer Supreme**. Though his life didn't turn out exactly how he expected, he found fulfillment in his work as **DOCTOR STRANGE**

CHAPTER 1

"**C**oming through!" shouted **Falcon** as he zoomed through the Long Island Mall. During his adventures as Falcon, Sam Wilson had seen some pretty crazy things. He had fought Super-Androids, alien armies, and even rock trolls. Now a group of werewolf-lizard creatures was invading, and he couldn't believe his weird luck. Falcon landed safely in the middle of the mall, where he met **Iron Man**, **Captain Marvel**, **Thor**, and **Scarlet Witch**. "Everyone

has been safely evacuated. The coast is clear,"
he said. "Let's go kick some werelizard butt.
Avengers, assemble!"

"Not so fast, Sam," said Iron Man. "We've
got to figure out what these things are first. That
way we know exactly what we're dealing with."

"They're **big**, **ugly**, and they **stink**," Sam said. "What more do we need to know?"

A group of crazed werelizards emerged from the food court, where they'd been snacking on tacos. The glint in their eyes said they were still hungry, and the Avengers looked like they could be the creatures' next meal.

"Back, monsters!" hollered Thor. He swung his mighty hammer, **Mjölnir**, and launched it directly at the werelizards, knocking down a row of them with a single blow.

"Help!" someone cried from nearby.

"It sounds like we missed someone during the evacuation," said Carol Danvers, known to her teammates as **Captain Marvel**. "I'll handle this one."

She followed the voice to Poloski's Department Store, where a little girl was hiding behind a rack of clothing. "Don't worry, sweetheart, you're safe now," Captain Marvel assured her.

"Look out!" the little girl said, pointing at an approaching were-lizard.

Captain Marvel kicked the werelizard, causing it to stumble backward and get disoriented. "And now for the big finish," she said, grabbing the beast by its scruff and tossing it into the air.

"Gotcha!" said Falcon, catching

the werelizard and
flying away with it.
"Let's find a good place
for you to take a *bath*." He
dropped the creature in the mall
fountain, and returned to his friends.

"Thanks for the assist, Sam," said Captain
Marvel.

"That's what teamwork is all about," Falcon
said. Sam was so preoccupied that he didn't
notice two hungry werelizards sneaking up
behind him.

"I guess it's up to the *handsome*,
super-intelligent **Tony Stark** to save
the day, as usual," Iron Man said, using his repulsor rays to blast away the
sneaky werelizards and save Falcon.

"At least I'm good at it. Hey, Wanda, what do you make of these things?"

"These beasts are **unnatural**," said **Wanda Maximoff**, the Scarlet Witch. She tried using her chaos magic to decipher the origin of the werelizards, but came up empty. "They've been enchanted with a strange magic even *my* power can't seem to figure out," she confessed.

"**Magic.** My *favorite*," Iron Man said, rolling his eyes. It was widely known that technology

lover Iron Man despised magic.

But there was one person who would know exactly where the werelizards came from. The only problem was that he didn't always see eye to eye with the Avengers—or any other heroes, for that matter—since they called him only when they needed something. He had a reputation for being aloof and difficult, though his power was undeniable. He was **Doctor Strange**, a master of the mystic arts. And it was only a matter of time before he showed up.

As the Avengers continued to fight the were-lizards, a familiar voice echoed through the mall: "These are curious little monsters. I wonder who made them."

"Show yourself, Loki," snarled Thor. "We haven't time for your games!"

In a puff of mist, **Loki**, Asgardian god of mischief, appeared. He hovered above the heroes, watching them battle and smirking.

"These disgusting creatures are *your* doing, aren't they, Brother?" said Thor.

"I would never create beasts *this* primitive. I simply came here to watch." Loki cackled.

Thor charged at his brother. He wasn't in the mood for this. **"Defend yourself!"** he shouted.

"Perhaps I'll visit again when you're less busy," said Loki, before disappearing in a burst of thin smoke.

Suddenly, the mall fell completely dark and a rumbling shook the structure to its foundation.

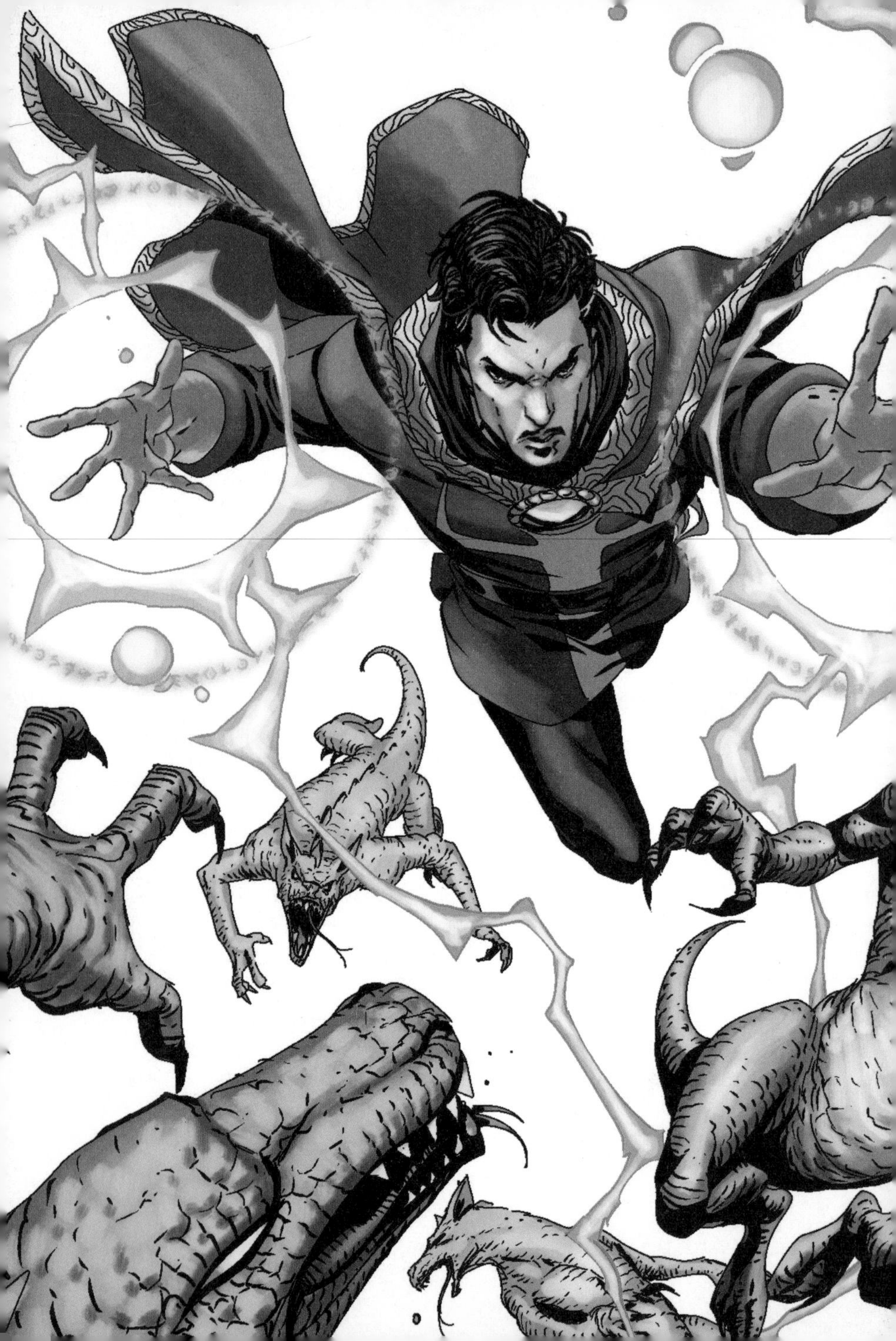

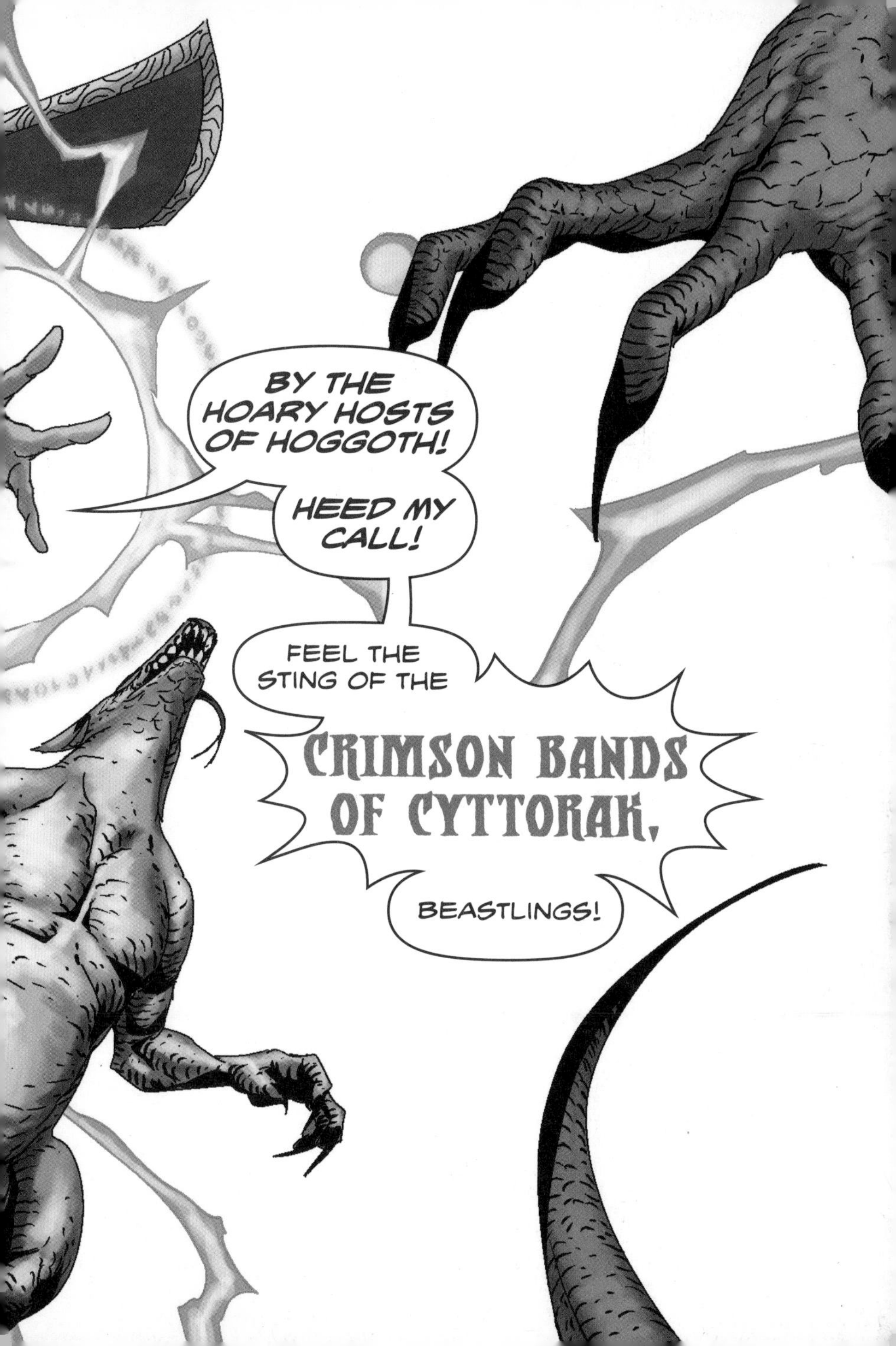
BY THE HOARY HOSTS OF HOGGOTH!
HEED MY CALL!
FEEL THE STING OF THE
CRIMSON BANDS OF CYTTORAK,
BEASTLINGS!

In a flash of lightning, each one disappeared right before their eyes, leaving behind only a wisp of vapor. The werelizards were gone at last, and things could return to normal. The Avengers stood amazed. Doctor Strange was quite impressive.

"It took you long enough," said Iron Man. "But thanks for the wacky magic mumbo jumbo. That was a close one."

"Believe it or not, *Mr. Stark*, I have matters of my own to attend to," said Doctor Strange. "You should know that magic is nothing to be trifled with."

"What *were* those things?" asked Captain Marvel.

"They were innocent animals who had been fused together," Strange explained. "I used a spell to transport them to another dimension, where they'll do no harm. When the spell wears off, they will return to their true forms and rejoin our world."

"**It was Loki!**" declared Thor.

Doctor Strange closed his eyes. He used his power as **Sorcerer Supreme** to reach out across the enchanted realms

and find information on the werelizards. Strange opened his eyes and they glowed bright yellow.

"This wasn't Loki's doing," he said. "It's a **dark magic** I cannot identify." Strange was very knowledgeable about magic in all its forms. If *he* couldn't identify the source of the disturbance, it did not bode well.

"Join the Avengers and we shall find this evil sorcery together," said Thor.

Strange brushed aside the offer. "No, thank you. You do not know the mystic arts like I do. The world of magic can be very dangerous, as you have seen today. If we were to work together, you'd just be in the way," he said, using his **Cloak of Levitation** to rise into the air.

"But we're so fun to hang out with!" joked Iron Man. "I'll even let you teach me a card trick or two."

"Mr. Stark, I prefer to handle magical affairs *on my own*. Farewell, Avengers," Doctor Strange declared, then disappeared into thin air.

Iron Man shook his head in disbelief. "Who turns down help from the Avengers?" he asked. "Oh well. Good luck, Doc. If something bad really *is* happening in the world of magic, *you're going to need it*."

CHAPTER 2

"I'm covered in the foul stench of **dark magic**!" shouted Doctor Strange, brushing himself off. He'd returned home with many questions. Someone was using magic for evil purposes, and he intended to find out who.

Doctor Strange's home, **the Sanctum Sanctorum**, was an enchanted mansion on a quiet street in **Manhattan's Greenwich Village**. No one would ever suspect it was filled with mysteries. Doctor Strange felt quite at home among its many magical curiosities.

As he made his way down a long hallway toward the library, he passed numerous mystical wonders. Each door in the Sanctum led to a different realm—some of them peaceful, some of them dangerous. Opening the wrong one could unleash a fleet of tentacled demons or the restless spirits of the undead.

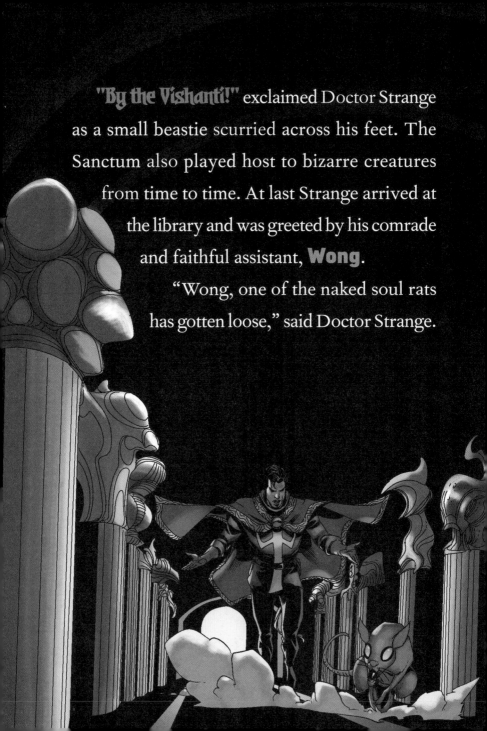

"**By the Vishanti!**" exclaimed Doctor Strange as a small beastie scurried across his feet. The Sanctum also played host to bizarre creatures from time to time. At last Strange arrived at the library and was greeted by his comrade and faithful assistant, **Wong**.

"Wong, one of the naked soul rats has gotten loose," said Doctor Strange.

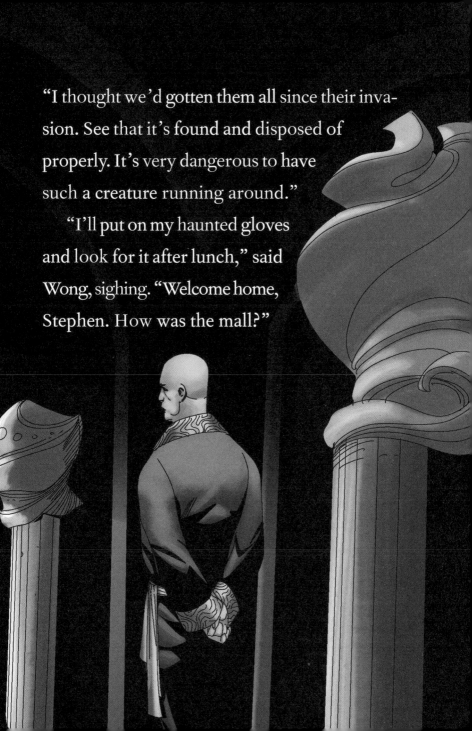

"I thought we'd gotten them all since their invasion. See that it's found and disposed of properly. It's very dangerous to have such a creature running around."

"I'll put on my haunted gloves and look for it after lunch," said Wong, sighing. "Welcome home, Stephen. How was the mall?"

Wong knew Doctor Strange better than anyone. They'd been confidants for many years, and Wong was always there to listen or offer advice when the world of magic was too much for Doctor Strange to handle. Wong was also an expert martial artist and master of all trades who cataloged Doctor Strange's many magical artifacts from across the multiverse.

"Something **BAD** is happening, Wong. The world of magic is in danger. Dark forces are at work, and

I must find the source before it's too late!" declared a frustrated Doctor Strange.

"I hope you didn't track ectoplasm across the floor when you arrived," said Wong. "I just cleaned all the rugs by hand." Wong was also the Sanctum's housekeeper.

"No, no, *no*," muttered Doctor Strange under his breath. It had been a long day, and he was getting extremely cranky. Strange's **Cloak of Levitation** whipped off of his body and hung itself neatly on a coatrack nearby as he began searching the bookshelves for information that could help.

"Relax. Take a hot bath. Are you hungry?" asked Wong. "I made some **soup**." Wong made a *very* tasty chicken noodle soup.

Strange wasn't having *any* of it. "I don't have time for baths and soup!" he exclaimed, furiously scanning his library. With so much information at his disposal, surely he'd be able to find the answers to his questions.

An idea occurred to him. "I must travel to the Astral Plane and speak with my mentor, the Ancient One. *He'll* be able to tell me about these dimensional fluctuations."

The Astral Plane was an alternate dimension beyond the earth, filled with magical energies both light and dark. To reach the Astral Plane, a magician must separate mind from body through

a process called astral projection. It required
focus and concentration.

Doctor Strange sat, legs crossed, in the middle
of the room. He closed his eyes tightly, took two
deep breaths, and cleared his mind. His journey
to the spirit world had begun.

"Be *careful*," warned Wong.

"I'm always careful," Doctor Strange assured him as his glowing blue spirit left his physical body and rose into the air.

Wong left Strange to his business. "I'll go see if I can find that soul rat," he said, leaving the room and closing the door behind him.

"Welcome, Stephen. It's been a long time. You're looking agitated," said the Ancient One, joining Doctor Strange on the Astral Plane. The Ancient One was a powerful magician of the highest order. He had been the Sorcerer Supreme *before* Doctor Strange inherited the title. When the Ancient One's mortal body passed on, his spirit moved to the Astral Plane for all eternity. Now whenever Doctor Strange needed advice, he visited his former instructor. They had an amiable but complicated relationship.

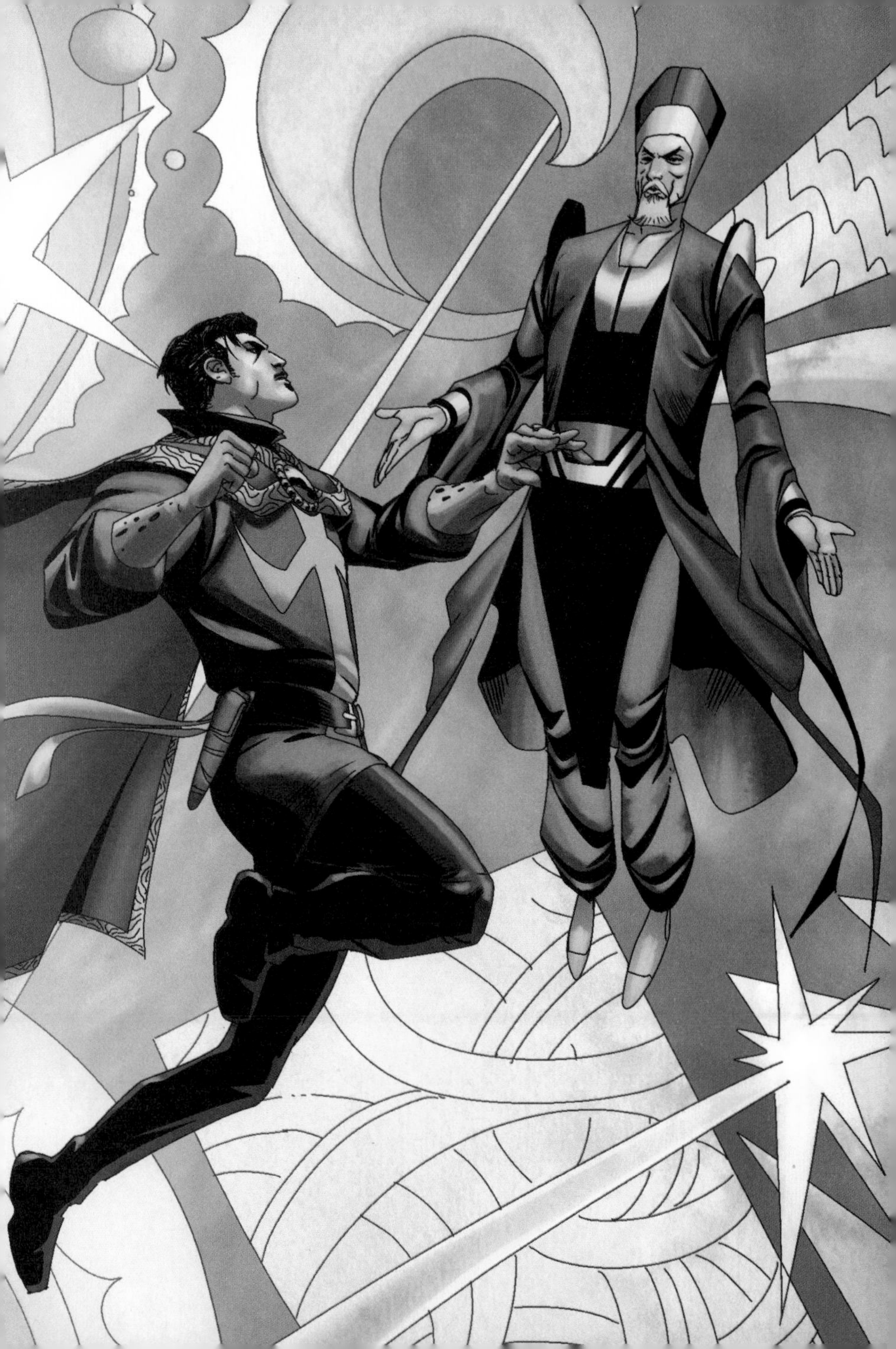

"I have no time for small talk. I need your *guidance*, Ancient One. Magic is being used unnaturally. Evil forces are at work," explained Doctor Strange. "What do you know of it?"

"Hmmm. You have many tools at your disposal. Look at all these spell books and enchanted weapons," the Ancient One said. "Why not use them?"

"I will," answered Strange. "But first I need help in finding the source of these troubles. I can sense danger, but I don't know where it's coming from."

"You have many enemies," offered the Ancient One.

"This is true. **Loki** could be a suspect, though the creatures I fought today aren't his style," said Strange. "I need more information."

"Have you tried asking your *friends* for assistance?" inquired the Ancient One. Doctor Strange bristled at the question.

"**The Avengers** are brightly colored Super Heroes whom I greatly respect," Strange explained, "but they don't understand the world of magic as I do. And I prefer to work *alone*."

The Ancient One eyed Strange's brightly colored **Cloak of Levitation** and let out a hearty chuckle. **"Ha-ha! Says the man with the dramatic living cape."** He smirked. **"I wasn't referring to the Avengers. *Friends* come in many shapes and sizes. You may *need* some in the near future."**

Doctor Strange disagreed. "I prefer to handle issues of magic by myself!" he demanded. "I come to you with important questions, and you answer me in riddles!"

"Calm yourself, master of the mystic arts. The Astral Plane is crawling with spirits who would take advantage of your emotion," warned the Ancient One. "You face *many* enemies, Stephen. Look around you and remain guarded. Life is a journey. Be *patient* and careful."

The Ancient One's spirit disappeared, and Doctor Strange was left alone on the Astral Plane. He thought his wise mentor would give him answers, but Strange was just left with more questions. As he prepared to return to the Earthly Plane, he sensed something was wrong. The Astral Plane grew cold, and a shiver shot up his spine. *He was not alone.*

CHAPTER 3

"How many lives have you saved, Stephen?" a soft voice whispered into Doctor Strange's ear, startling him. He turned to see who it could be, but no one was there. Someone new was with him on the Astral Plane. The voice grew angry. "Master of the mystic arts? HA! You are not worthy of the power you wield!"

Doctor Strange felt uneasy. The voice sounded familiar but he couldn't quite place it. Even in his astral form, Strange could feel the room

getting colder. Dark shadows danced across the walls in front of him. "Show yourself, whoever you are!" he shouted. Soon the shadows began peeling away to become slithering snakelike creatures. **"By the Vishanti,"** he muttered under his breath.

"The Vishanti can't help you now," the mysterious voice replied.

The shadow creatures taunted Strange as their hissing grew louder and louder. Sensing danger, the Cloak of Levitation quickly surrounded

Doctor Strange's physical body, shielding it from danger. "Let the light of the all-seeing Eye of Agamotto blind you, creatures of the dark!" Strange ordered sternly. The cloak's amulet released a flash of blinding white light, burning the shadow creatures and causing them to sizzle. They scattered back into the walls, but the whispers continued.

"You doubt yourself, Strange. I see magic is taking its toll on you," the voice said. "Why not relax and take the vacation of your dreams?"

At last! Doctor Strange knew exactly who he was dealing with: **Nightmare**, ruler of the **Dream Dimension**. Nightmare was a ghoulish villain who delighted in tormenting his enemies with their deepest and darkest fears. He wished to feed on those fears and use them to increase his power. He often hid on the Astral Plane, lying in wait to strike Strange at his weakest moment. He was close to getting his wish.

"Do not mock me, Nightmare!" commanded Doctor Strange. The shadow creatures appeared again, swarming Strange's astral form from behind and grabbing him tightly. He struggled to break free, but their grip tightened.

At last, **Nightmare** showed himself. He stared at Doctor Strange, tilting his head ever so slightly. He was looking for **fear**. Nightmare

snapped his fingers and a vision of the past appeared in front of Doctor Strange. It was an
image of his early days as a young doctor. It
had brought him great joy to save lives using
the skills he learned in medical school, but a
terrible accident had changed all that. He lost
the use of his hands and was no longer able to
perform surgery. It hurt Strange to be reminded
of his past in such a way.

"My powers have grown since last we tangled," Nightmare sneered. "Look at your past, Stephen. See your fear. See your pain!" The happy visions swiftly became darker. Doctor Strange watched his younger self grow frustrated, struggling to hold a scalpel. It made him angry.

"You won't scare *me*, Nightmare. I fought through my pain. It made me stronger," Strange growled. "And when I break free, I'll show you *just* how strong I've become."

Nightmare let out a loud belly laugh, savoring the moment. Strange, however, saw an opportunity. He looked around the room, scanning it for items he could use to escape. *Aha!* The Sword of Ultimate Shadow would do the trick. It was housed in a glass case nearby. Strange focused his mental energies and commanded the sword to leap from the case and cut him out of the shadow creatures' grip. The sword did just that, and soon Doctor Strange's astral form was free at last. He grabbed the weapon and gripped it tightly, preparing for battle.

"Clever, clever," said Nightmare. "Your magical items come in quite handy. I hope no one ever steals them. Then you'd be in real trouble."

Could Nightmare be behind the dark magic Doctor Strange had sensed? He was certainly powerful enough; that much was obvious. "The world of magic is unbalanced. What do you know of it?" demanded Strange.

Nightmare cackled heartily once again. "Ha-ha-ha! Magic is always unbalanced! Magic is always uncertain! That is its nature, FOOL!"

Doctor Strange became impatient. "Why are you here, Nightmare? Reveal your *true* intentions or leave the Astral Plane at once!"

"My intentions were simply to test your mettle," said Nightmare. "You'll soon face a much bigger challenge than I present. The question remains: Will you rise to the occasion?"

Nightmare slithered his thin frame through the air toward Doctor Strange. "Your fears were delicious. I look forward to dining on them again soon," he said before evaporating.

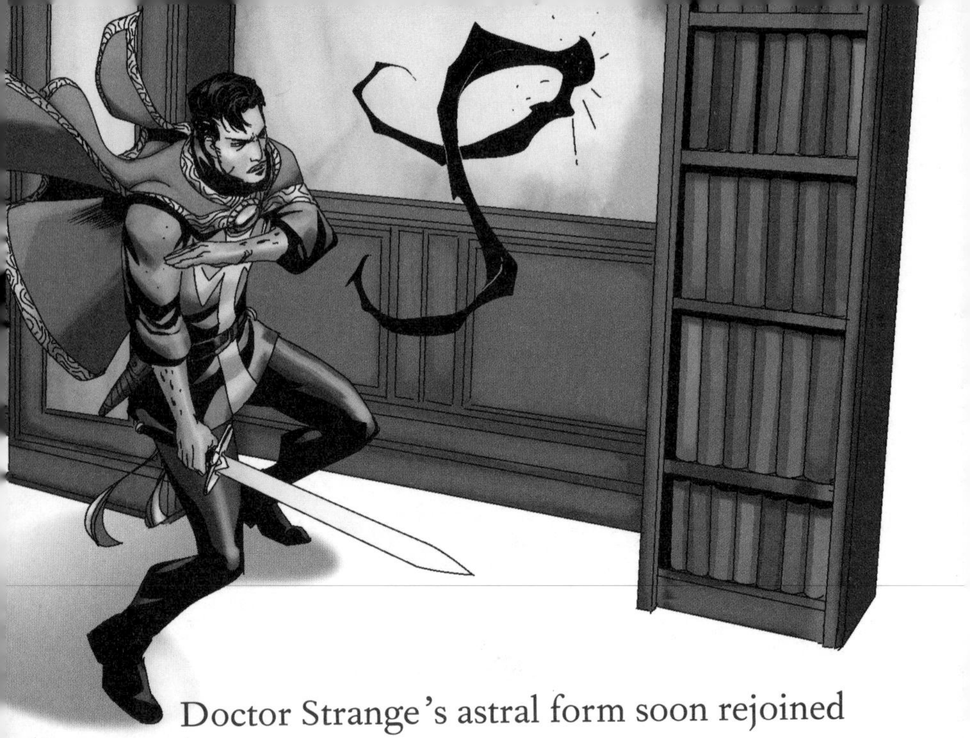

Doctor Strange's astral form soon rejoined his physical body as he returned to the Earthly Plane. He was exhausted by Nightmare's taunting. In fact, it had made him quite hungry.

Wong sensed his friend was in need and rushed into the room to check on him. "Are you all right?" he asked. "I heard some commotion."

"I'm fine," replied Strange, out of breath. "I think I'll have some of that **SOUP** now."

CHAPTER 4

"You have visitors!" yelled Wong.

Doctor Strange had been reading **the Book of the Vishanti** for days. It contained powerful spells that Strange could use to defend himself against a variety of attacks, but would it be *enough*? The same question had been bothering him since the incident with the werelizards: *What is happening to magic?* For the moment, it would remain unanswered as he attended to some unexpected guests.

"May I present the **Scarlet Witch** and **Iron Fist**," announced Wong, taking an extravagant bow. "Welcome to **the Sanctum Sanctorum**."

"I guess we're pretty important, huh?" said Iron Fist.

"Wong is putting on a *show* for you," said Strange. Wong had quite a sense of humor. "**Daniel Rand**, otherwise known as **Iron Fist**, Zen student of the **K'un Lun**. It's a pleasure to meet you. **Wanda Maximoff**, the **Scarlet Witch**, good to see you again. What brings you by? I'm *very* busy."

"We were just in the neighborhood and wanted to hang out. Let's order pizza!" said Iron Fist, plopping down in a chair and putting up his feet.

The Scarlet Witch smiled. "Your home is truly amazing, Stephen. My powers aren't *nearly* as developed as yours, but I'd love to spend some time in your library," she said, gazing at the many marvels that surrounded her. "I envy your commitment."

"You are an incredible illusionist, Wanda," complimented Strange. "Focus on your strengths and not your weaknesses. Only then can you grow."

The arms of Iron Fist's chair reared up and grabbed him by the wrists, causing him to jump. **"WHOA!"** he exclaimed. "That chair is *alive*!"

"Indeed it is," said Doctor Strange. "The Sanctum is filled with many enchanted relics from my adventures across the dimensional planes. And yet even with all of these items, I can't find the answers I currently need."

Iron Fist picked up a bizarre-looking cylinder and began to play with it as if he were a pirate with a sword.

"What's *this* do?" he asked. "I bet it's a magic toilet plunger!"

"PUT THAT DOWN. *That* is **the Wand of Watoomb,** and it is *not* a toy," warned Doctor Strange. "What is the *purpose* of the visit, Scarlet Witch? I needn't be a magician to sense that you're not here to merely *hang out*."

Scarlet Witch was a little embarrassed. She couldn't fool Doctor Strange. "Someone is manipulating mystic forces beyond our control," she said. "You and I have *both* sensed it, as has Iron Fist. I know you don't like working with others, but we want to help."

"I am the Sorcerer Supreme and a **master of the mystic arts**," replied Strange. "I don't *need* help, thank you."

"That doesn't protect you from *everything*," said Iron Fist. "What do you do when a bad guy tries to give you a good old-fashioned punch to the face?"

"Why don't we spar a bit, and I can show you?" Strange offered.

"**No way**. You'd probably use some magic on me when I wasn't looking," said Iron Fist.

Doctor Strange's Cloak of Levitation—with its amulet, the Eye of Agamotto—gently removed itself from his body and floated over to the corner, where it hovered patiently. "Now I'm without my magic vestments. Does *this* put your mind at ease?" he asked.

"That sounds like a *challenge* to me," said Scarlet Witch.

Iron Fist looked Doctor Strange square in the eye. They both nodded and the match began. The heroes circled each other patiently, considering exactly how to strike. It had been a while since Strange had sparred with someone other than Wong. It gave him quite a thrill.

"I like the gray streaks in your hair, *Steve*," said Iron Fist, smiling. "How *old* are you again?"

"I'm old enough to know what *trash talking* sounds like,"

Strange countered. "And *don't* call me *Steve*."

The two heroes sparred for quite a while, jabbing, hooking, and avoiding each other with relative ease.

Strange swept the leg of Iron Fist and forced him to the ground.

HI-YAH!

"Uncle?" asked Strange.

"Uncle!" replied Iron Fist. Strange released him, and Iron Fist rose to his feet. "You're good, Doc. I didn't see that one coming."

"And I didn't even have to use **the Bolts of Balthakk** to subdue you," said Strange with a smile. "Words of advice—both magic *and* fighting are about *misdirection*."

"Pretty wise stuff. Where'd you learn those moves, anyway?" asked Iron Fist.

"**Wong** isn't just a good cook; he's also a superb hand-to-hand combatant," offered Strange.

"Ah, so there's a *right* way and a *Wong* way?" joked Iron Fist.

Scarlet Witch had a curious look on her face as she glanced around the room at Doctor Strange's enchanted weaponry. "With so many powerful items in one place, how do you keep the Sanctum safe from outside forces?" she asked.

"I've installed numerous magical protections in order to safeguard the Sanctum from extradimensional danger. No one can enter the Sanctum unless given permission by myself or Wong," said Doctor Strange. "One should be prepared for the unexpected."

Wong rushed into the room with news. "I hate to interrupt, but **vampires** are attacking **Grand Central Station**. I thought you might want to do something about it," he said. "I also made some tea if anyone is thirsty."

"Another disturbance I couldn't foresee!" exclaimed Doctor Strange. "I've got to get to Grand Central at once."

"We'll join you," offered Scarlet Witch.

"No," countered Doctor Strange. "That won't be necessary. Stay here. Have a cup of Wong's tea." Doctor Strange held out his arms, welcoming **the Cloak of Levitation** and **Eye of Agamotto** back onto his body. "It's time for me to get to work."

CHAPTER 5

"By the Hoary Hosts of Hoggoth!" exclaimed Doctor Strange. He had arrived at **Grand Central Station** to find vampires frightening travelers and wreaking havoc. Strange despised **vampires** and considered them nasty, ruthless bloodsuckers.

He scanned the area with his mystic power and noticed something peculiar. These vampires weren't looking for blood at all. They were focused only on scaring people. *This is bizarre*, he thought.

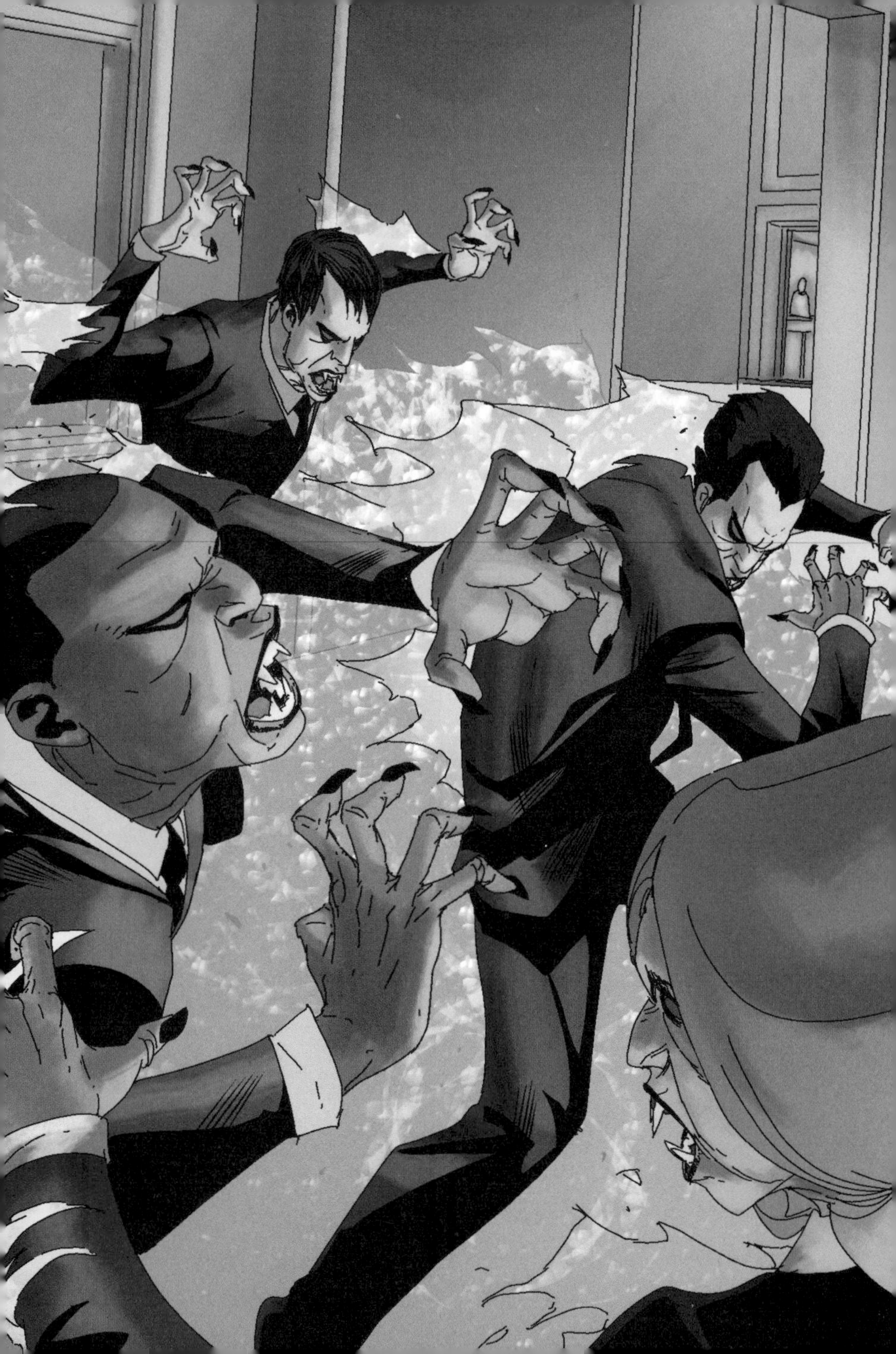

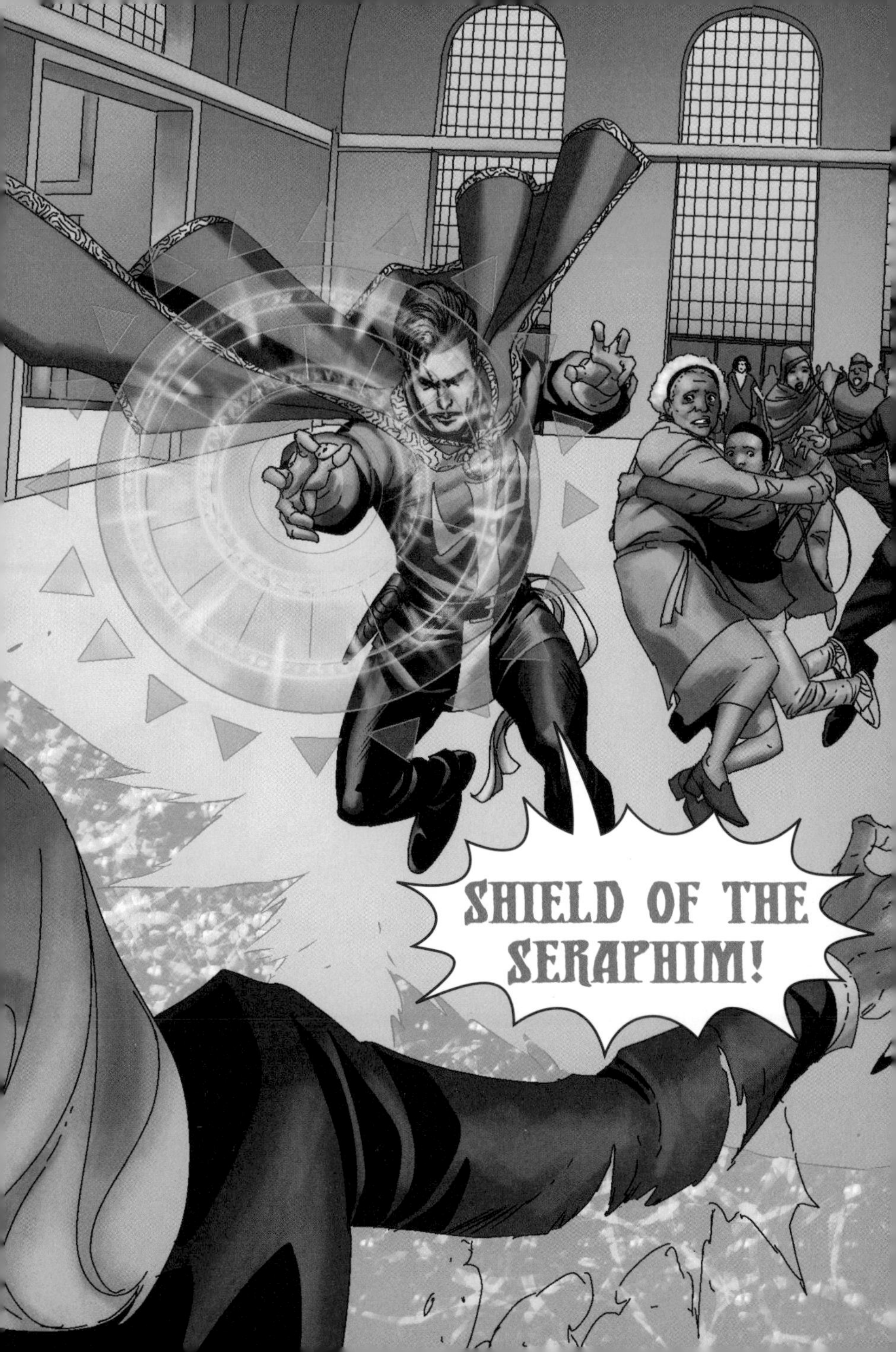
SHIELD OF THE SERAPHIM!

Doctor Strange created a protective barrier, shielding the frightened passengers. The vampires struck the shield and, realizing it was impossible to break through, ran away in defeat.

"Thank you, Mister Magic," a boy said.

"You're welcome. Now be a hero and help your grandmother, young man," said Strange. "You'll be safe outside."

The young boy took off as Strange heard the sound of battle nearby. Someone was fighting vampires alone.

As he moved to get a closer look, Strange
discovered it was the hero known as White
Tiger. She'd been taking down vampires
for a while and was losing steam quickly.

"How about a hand over here?" White
Tiger asked, punching a vampire right
in the face.

"The mystical tiger amulet, is
it yours?" asked Strange.

"It sure is," said White
Tiger. "How about some
magic, if you don't mind?"

Doctor Strange
raised his hands
high in the air as
his eyes glowed
a bright yellow.

CRYSTALS OF CYNDRIARR! he bellowed, and hundreds of daggerlike crystals rained down on the attacking vampires, causing them to flee.

"Thanks," said White Tiger, brushing herself off and taking a moment to catch her breath. "These things just appeared out of nowhere and started causing trouble. They're not biting anyone on the neck, so *that's* good. I think

someone is just trying to wear us out."

Doctor Strange was impressed. "That's a keen observation," he said. "There is disorder in the world of magic. Someone or *something* is meddling in forces beyond their control." White Tiger's amulet began to glow. "The talisman that you wear. It's very curious and powerful."

"It's how I get my powers," explained White

Tiger. "You can take a look at it sometime, but only if you promise to give me some magical training."

The idea excited Doctor Strange. "Attune yourself to the amulet's power. Use it to clear your mind and focus your abilities. Then you'll be able to—" He hesitated, sensing trouble nearby.

"AHHH!" A cry rang out. Vampires were closing in again, and someone needed help.

White Tiger scanned the area. Her enhanced senses came in handy during situations like this.

"I'd love to stay and chat, but I've got work to do," she said, before diving into a sea of angry vampires.

Strange studied White Tiger as she fought. Her amulet not only gave her strength and agility, but it allowed her to focus on tasks without distraction. *That's a valuable asset, especially for someone as young as she*, he thought.

The vampires were dwindling in number, but it was time for the big finish. Doctor Strange wondered how he could take them all out at once. He used his mystic power to scan them again. This time something astonishing was revealed. The vampires were actually hollow shells made entirely of **magic**. Since they weren't living creatures, Strange could do anything he wanted to destroy them.

SEVEN SUNS OF CINNIBUS!

he shouted, calling forth a rain of heat and light. It zapped all the vampires with sharp bolts of lightning, causing them to crumble into ash. Grand Central Station was at last vampire-free.

White Tiger was impressed. "That was **awesome!**" she said. "I hope I never have to fight a bunch of **gross** vampires again. Thanks for the help."

"Be glad they weren't **Mind Maggots**," Strange said. "And you're welcome."

"I'm not used to working with other Super Heroes," White Tiger explained. "Well, except **Spider-Man**. And **Nova**. Oh, and **Iron Fist**. I guess what I mean to say is, thanks. I couldn't have done this without your help. We should do it again sometime."

"Perhaps we should. *Anyone* who can stand the company of Iron Fist deserves my respect and admiration," Strange joked. As he left White Tiger and headed back to the Sanctum, Strange wondered if maybe he'd been wrong about working with other heroes.

Was it time for a change?

CHAPTER 6

Doctor Strange was exhausted. He calmly soared through the clouds above New York City, but his mind was racing. He was puzzled by the sudden and bizarre assaults that had been happening in and around the city. Strange's magical senses were thrown off, and he couldn't make sense of things. Every time he thought he had the answer, a new question arose.

It was time once again for him to visit the Astral Plane and seek the counsel of **the Ancient One**.

Strange found a nice quiet place behind a cloud where no one would bother him. Clearing his mind as best he could, his spirit form awoke and joined **the Astral Plane**. The Ancient One was waiting for him.

"It's good to see you again, Stephen," he said. **"I imagine you have more questions for me that I cannot possibly answer."**

"I *demand* answers!" commanded Strange.

"Do *not* make demands of me, Sorcerer Supreme!" boomed the Ancient One. The loud outburst shook even the peaceful clouds. The Ancient One was a benevolent being, but he also had a temper, especially when his authority was questioned.

Doctor Strange sighed. He hadn't meant to snap at his trusted mentor, but he was simply at his wits' end. "The bridge between the natural world and the world of magic is breaking down," he said. "I've fought animals that were crudely fused together and hollow vampires who attacked without purpose. **Nightmare** showed me my greatest fears, and **Loki** may be involved. What does it all mean? Is this a test, Ancient One? Are these incidents connected? Nothing makes sense." Strange was deeply frustrated, and it showed.

"Such dramatic talk for a doctor," said the Ancient One. **"*Everything* is a test, Stephen. Calm yourself. Clear your mind. You're looking for obvious answers where none may be found."**

"More riddles," grumbled Strange. "I should

have *expected* more riddles. You're one of the most powerful magicians I have ever known. You are wise beyond recollection, and yet you have *no answers!*"

"You are correct!" agreed the Ancient One. **"It's up to *you* to take a hard look at the patterns and figure out how the pieces fit together. Only you can provide the answers. You are surrounded by allies and yet you resist their assistance. Why?"**

Doctor Strange was getting frustrated again. "I don't *need* their assistance! I don't need *anyone's* assistance. I am the Sorcerer Supreme and a master of the mystic arts. I should be able to handle anything and everything that concerns the world of magic *on my own.*"

"And yet, here you are," the Ancient One stated firmly.

He has a point, thought Strange. *If I were really so powerful, I would have been able to find a way to solve this problem already.*

"Do not resist the counsel of your colleagues and friends. Their advice is valuable," said the Ancient One. "New perspectives must *always* be welcomed. You may find them in the least likely of places."

Strange considered the Ancient One's words as an astral earthquake shook them both. Strange focused on locating the source of the trouble. "The Museum of Natural History!" he exclaimed. It was time to take care of business. "Thank you, Ancient One. I believe the path is becoming clearer to me."

"A wise man knows there's always something new to learn." And with that, the Ancient One's spirit form evaporated.

Doctor Strange thought deeply about what **the Ancient One** had said. A new perspective was *just* what he needed.

Strange used his consciousness to search the Astral Plane for someone who could help. Finally, he found the person he was looking for: **Jericho Drumm**, otherwise known as **Brother Voodoo**.

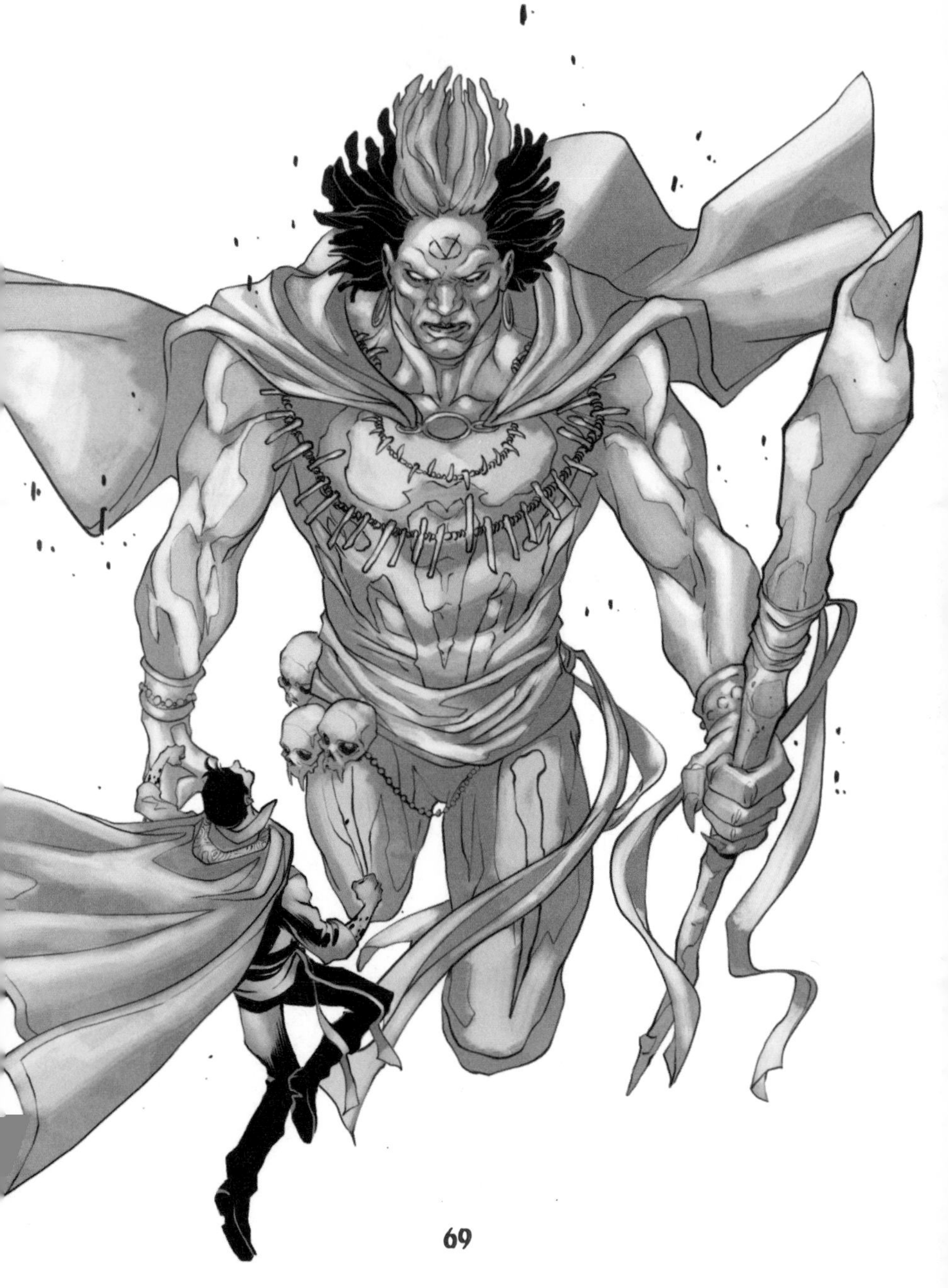

Strange had met **Brother Voodoo** many years before, when they were young magicians. Much had changed in their lives since then.

"Pardon me, Jericho," Strange interrupted. "It's been a long time."

"It has indeed. Hello, Doctor Strange," said Brother Voodoo. "If **the Sorcerer Supreme** is reaching out to me, something big must be happening. What can I do for you?"

"Meet me at the Museum of Natural History," answered Strange. "You and I are going demon hunting."

CHAPTER

7

Doctor Strange was standing in the middle of the Museum, feeling out of place. He'd been waiting for **Brother Voodoo** for over ten minutes and was beginning to get annoyed.

"Excuse me, but do you work here?" a tourist woman asked him. Her little boy looked him up and down, admiring **the Cloak of Levitation**.

"No, madam, I do *not* work here. I am a *doctor*," said Strange, forcing a smile. *I should have made myself invisible*, he thought. "If you'll excuse

me, I must attend to some business."

Doctor Strange grew nervous as the woman reached into her purse. With so many unexpected occurrences lately, she could've very well been an evil sorceress in disguise. He braced himself for whatever was coming next.

"Would you mind taking a photo of me and my son?" the woman asked sheepishly.

"Mom, can the doctor be in the photo, too?" the boy asked. **"I like his cape!"**

Doctor Strange awkwardly posed with the woman and her son. They thanked him and went on their merry way. *That wasn't so bad*, Strange thought. He received a few lingering stares, but was otherwise ignored by the museum-goers. In New York City, a man wearing a flowing red cloak wasn't as weird as people might've thought.

"Taking photographs with fans?" said Brother Voodoo, appearing out of thin air. "I had no idea that a master of the mystic arts did such things."

Brother Voodoo had known Doctor Strange for many years. Their paths, though often very

different, had crossed numerous times. **Jericho Drumm** gained his powers by joining himself to the spirit of his dying brother and studying voodoo under a mystic priest known as a *houngan*. He eventually became an expert in **dark magic** and used his powers to communicate with the **spirits of the dead**, an ability Strange had trouble mastering. Voodoo's powers could be unpredictable, which made Strange slightly uneasy. But the two heroes had much to offer each other and delighted in the opportunity to work together.

"It's good to see you, Voodoo," said Strange. "I want you to know that any competition we may have had in the past is of little consequence now. We are both *experts* in the field of magic, and I respect you very much." Strange paused.

He looked around and saw that no one seemed to notice Brother Voodoo's presence.

"I'm invisible to everyone in the museum except for *you*. It's better this way," explained Voodoo. He'd brought along a host of mystical items, including shrunken heads, **the Staff of Legba**, and assorted magic powders. "It's not so easy for someone dressed like *I* am to walk right through the front door. How'd *you* get in?"

"I'm a member, of course. I have always found natural history to be quite *fascinating*," clarified Strange. He waved his hand fancifully, making himself invisible. "Now we're *both* cloaked and can focus on the task at hand. Did you bring your powders?"

Voodoo motioned to his utility belt, filled with trinkets and magic dusts. "I brought them all," he said. He poured a thimbleful of sparkling red powder into Strange's hand.

Strange tossed the powder into the air and blew it across the crowd. As it settled, his suspicions were confirmed. The museum was crawling with **demon elves**. They'd been skulking around in secret and seemed confused.

"Can they see us?" asked Voodoo.

"No," replied Strange. "They seem to be trapped between realms, with no means of escape. I believe they came here, to the museum,

looking for something they could use to return
home."

"Are they dangerous?" asked Voodoo.

"They're **demon elves**," offered Strange.
"They're certainly not our friends."

Voodoo pondered the predicament. "This
is a tricky situation indeed. These creatures are
lost, without a way home," he said. "They may
be **demons**, but so far they haven't hurt anyone

or caused trouble. It would be foolish to engage them in battle at this point. We must remove them from this plane of existence without revealing ourselves. First and foremost, we'll need to keep the people safe."

Doctor Strange was very impressed with Brother Voodoo. Normally, Strange followed his own instincts and did things *his* way. It was rare for him to listen to the advice of others.

Perhaps working together wasn't so bad after all. It gave him an idea.

"I know a spell we can use to remove the demon elves," said Strange. "It's quite unpleasant and could frighten the creatures into violence. I'll need your help to control it and make sure that doesn't happen."

"And you shall have it, Doctor," assured Voodoo. "I'll hypnotize these beasts so they remain silent and peaceful."

Voodoo began to murmur secret spells. He raised **the Staff of Legba** in the air and shook it vigorously. As it glowed bright with mystic power, the demons stopped in their tracks to look at its radiant light.

Now it was time for Doctor Strange to work his magic. His body pulsed with mystic energies ready to be harnessed. The spell he had in mind was usually used for *attacking* demons. Using it to *help* demons would take every ounce of control he had. Strange was nervous as he focused his power. The barrier between realms was fragile, and they both knew how important it was to protect it. Voodoo noticed Strange trembling and sweating quite a bit. His magic was breaking down.

Suddenly, a headstrong **demon elf** shook itself out of its peaceful trance and shrieked deafeningly. The screech soon roused the other demon elves from their daze. They were awake, and they were *not* happy. Neither was Doctor Strange.

"Blast it!" Strange said angrily. **"I couldn't sustain my power. The barrier between**

worlds has broken down." Strange didn't like being so emotional in front of Voodoo, but he didn't have time to think about it—not with a horde of fuming demon elves standing before them.

"Take a moment to collect your thoughts, Stephen," said Voodoo. "Loa conceal us!" A dense fog swept into the room, camouflaging the magic heroes. But not before a nasty demon elf spotted them and charged at the weakened Doctor Strange. Brother Voodoo waved **the Staff of Legba**, creating a cage of protective fire and stopping the demon elf in its tracks.

"Now that these creatures are aware of our presence, we do not have much time, Doctor Strange," said Voodoo. Strange nodded. It was now or never.

Keep it together, Stephen, he thought. A gigantic glowing hand appeared above **the demon elves**. It carefully scooped them up and returned them to the dimension from which they had come. Doctor Strange let out a well-deserved sigh of relief. The process had gone smoother than he could have imagined.

"Thank you, Jericho. I *truly* appreciate your help," said Strange.

Without Brother Voodoo's expertise, the situation might've been much worse. It gave Strange an idea. It was time to end the magical assaults once and for all. "Join me on a new adventure, **Brother Voodoo**?" he asked. "I'll share a spell with you on the way there."

Brother Voodoo smiled. "Anything for a *friend*."

Belvedere Castle sat peacefully in the middle of **Central Park**, unaware that it would soon be the base of operations for a very important mission. Doctor Strange had sent out a magical message to his comrades, asking them to join him there. He wasn't quite sure if they would show up, but one by one they soon arrived: **Scarlet Witch**, **Iron Fist**, **White Tiger**, and **Brother Voodoo**.

The assembled heroes stood together as Doctor Strange addressed them. "As you know, there have been unexplained breaches in the barrier between our world and the beyond. Someone has been abusing creatures of **magic**. This must *stop*. I will continue to investigate the source of these crimes, but in the meantime, we must send *all* of these creatures back from whence they came."

The heroes looked at one another. It was an enormous responsibility. Doctor Strange continued. "Each of you is here because you have something special and important to share. You're *heroes*, and I can't think of anyone else whom I would rather work with to end this nightmare."

"I've got a question," said Iron Fist, raising his hand. "I thought you didn't like working with other people. What made you change your mind?"

White Tiger lightly jabbed Iron Fist in the ribs with her elbow. *"Rude,"* she said. "This guy is a doctor. Show him some respect."

"The truth is that I didn't think I needed any help. But then each of you showed me that sometimes solving problems requires teamwork," Strange answered. "You all have something unique to share, and *together* I believe we can accomplish great things."

"Sounds good to me!" said Iron Fist, smiling.

"What can we do to help?" asked Scarlet Witch.

"We're going to draw every single magical beast in New York City out of the darkness and assemble them right here. Then we're going to open a portal and drive them back from whence they came," Doctor Strange explained. "*First* **Brother Voodoo** will use his **Staff of Legba** to cast a spell, creating a beacon that draws all the beasts to this area. I will lend him some of my power to accomplish this. *Then* **Scarlet Witch** will use her chaos magic to open a dimensional portal that will send them all home." He turned to Scarlet Witch. "Wanda, you'll need to keep the portal open until every single creature has exited our world. It will be difficult to maintain and may put a strain on your powers. Are you up for it?"

"I'll do *whatever* it takes," she said confidently.

"What about White Tiger and **me**?" asked Iron Fist. "How are *we* going to help?"

"You both have a very important role," explained Strange. "Once the creatures begin to arrive, it's up to you to make sure they go straight through that portal. Your job requires patience and, most likely, force. Some of these beasts may resist, and things could become problematic. Thankfully, you're both skilled fighters."

"We won't let you down, Doc."

"If you'll all move into formation now, we

can begin the process," Doctor Strange declared. **"Vapors of Valtorr!"** A protective fog rolled in, shielding the heroes from prying eyes.

Brother Voodoo began his mystical chants. He held **the Staff of Legba** high as **Doctor Strange** infused it with some of his own power. Lightning from the heavens struck the staff as a loud **BOOM** echoed throughout the city. The magic staff pulsed with the power of one thousand suns. The magic flare began to draw out each and every enchanted beast in New York City. There were **werelizards**, **vampires**, and **shadow snakes**. Tiny **fairies** descended from the sky, and **zombies** rose from the ground. **Ghouls** of all kinds swarmed the park.

"Wanda, stand by to open the portal," Strange commanded. **"Now!"**

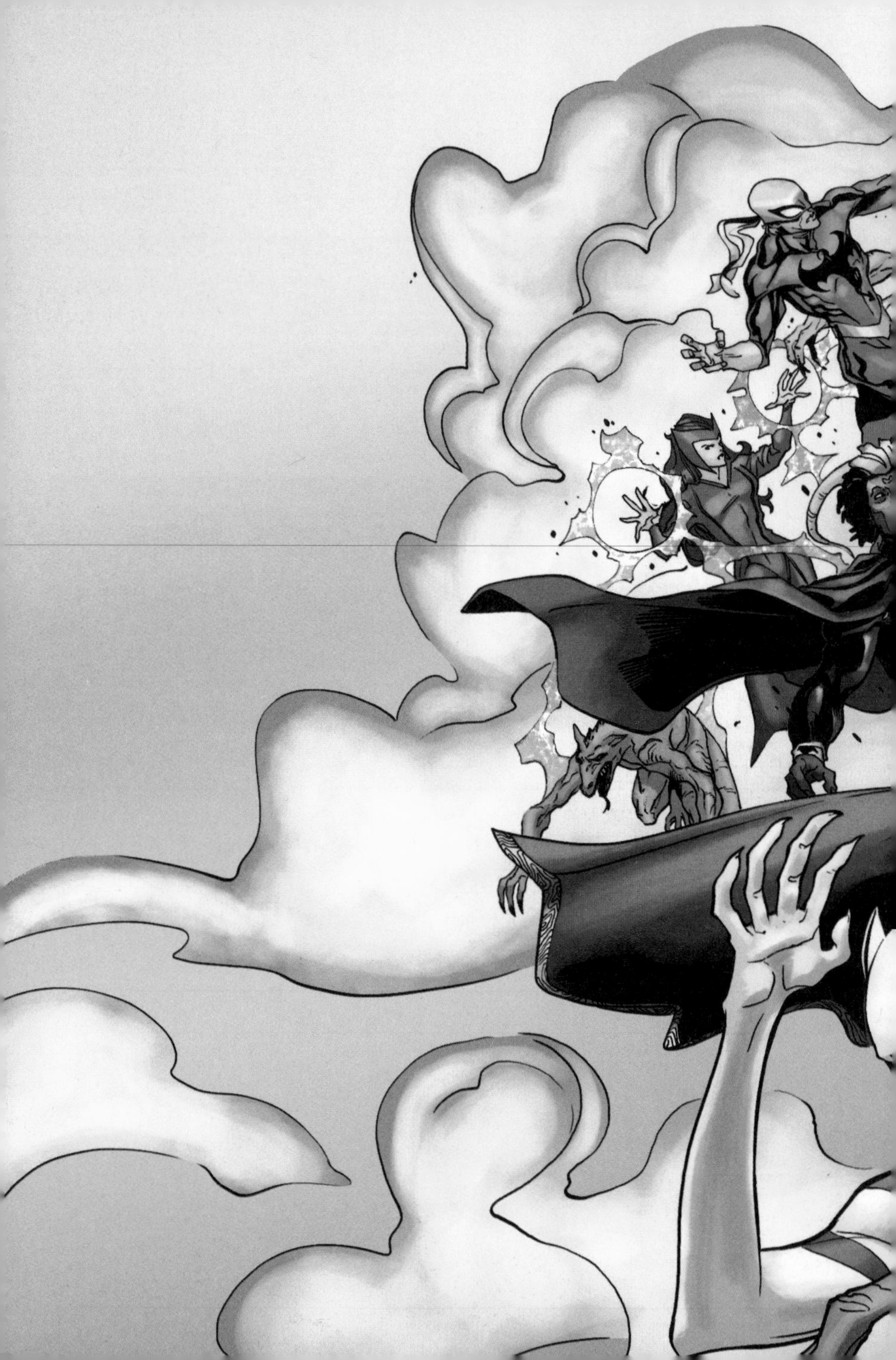

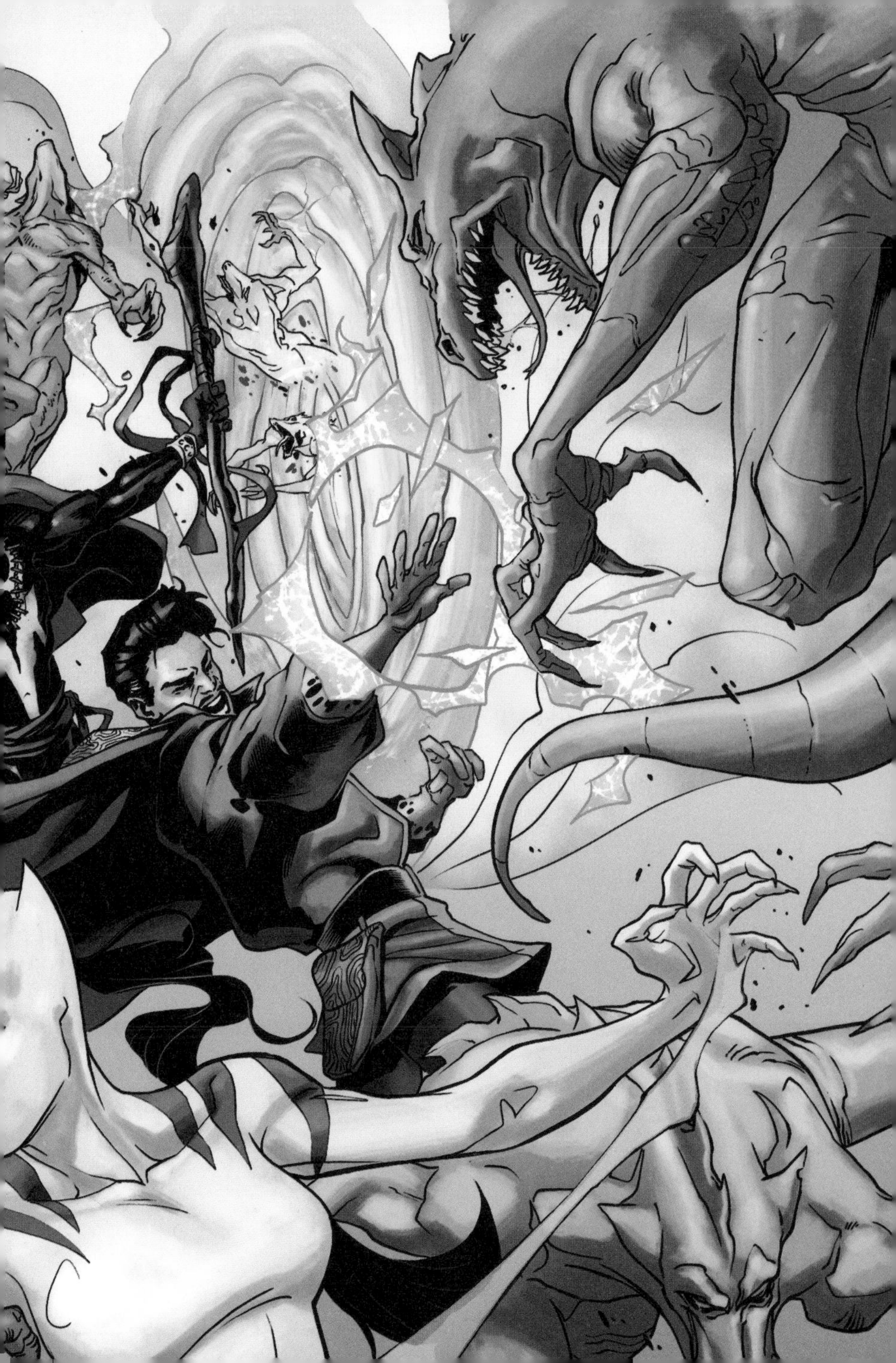

Scarlet Witch focused her chaos magic, opening a rift in time and space.

"All right, big guy, in you go!" said White Tiger, grabbing an angry **troll** and tossing him in. When a fight erupted between the **were-lizards** and the **vampires**, **Iron Fist** broke it up, sending all the creatures through the portal as well. Doctor Strange's plan seemed to be a success. But he wondered if perhaps it was all too good to be true.

Then the sky grew dark as an evil presence swept across the city. The doctor looked up to see a glowing message written in the clouds: **WHERE IS WONG?** Strange panicked. **"I must go!"**

CHAPTER 9

Doctor Strange burst through the doors of the Sanctum Sanctorum and was met with silence.

"WONG?" he shouted at the top of his lungs. Strange was worried. He frantically searched each room, using his powers to scan every inch of his home. Wong was *nowhere* to be found. Suddenly, the silence was broken. Laughter echoed throughout the Sanctum, and it had a familiar tone. *Loki* had arrived!

"LOKI! It was you all along," accused Strange.

"No, Sorcerer Supreme. *I'm* not the one who has been causing you so much trouble, but I know who has," Loki admitted. "*He's* about to arrive, and you will bow before his dark power!"

Doctor Strange was confused. "Why are you here, Loki? What's in it for you?"

Loki guffawed loudly. He was enjoying this. "My role was to distract you. I'm a *trickster*, after all. I desire that beautiful ax of yours," he said, motioning to the Ax of Angarruumus, hanging on the wall. "I need something big and threatening that will scare Thor." Loki sensed a change in the air. "Ah, yes. He's here now, and I must go. Good-bye, Doctor Strange. I look forward to your defeat." He vanished.

Doctor Strange felt the Sanctum getting hotter. Sweat began to drip from his brow. Now he knew exactly whom he was dealing with. It was one of his oldest and most dangerous enemies. **"REVEAL YOURSELF, SPAWN OF EVIL!"** shouted Strange.

A deep and frightening voice called out from beyond. **"It's over, Doctor Strange."** **The Flames of the Faltine** covered the walls of the Sanctum as **the Lord of Darkness**, **Eater of Souls**, emerged from the Dark Dimension. Strange's true enemy was revealed at last. **DORMAMMU!**

"How did you get past the Sanctum's magical protections?" asked Strange.

"Simple trickery. Magic is about misdirection; didn't you know?" taunted Dormammu. **"I disguised myself as you and showed up on the doorstep of the Sanctum wounded. Surely Wong wouldn't turn away his master when he needed him most."**

"Where is Wong?" asked Strange. He was angry but focused. To find Wong and save the

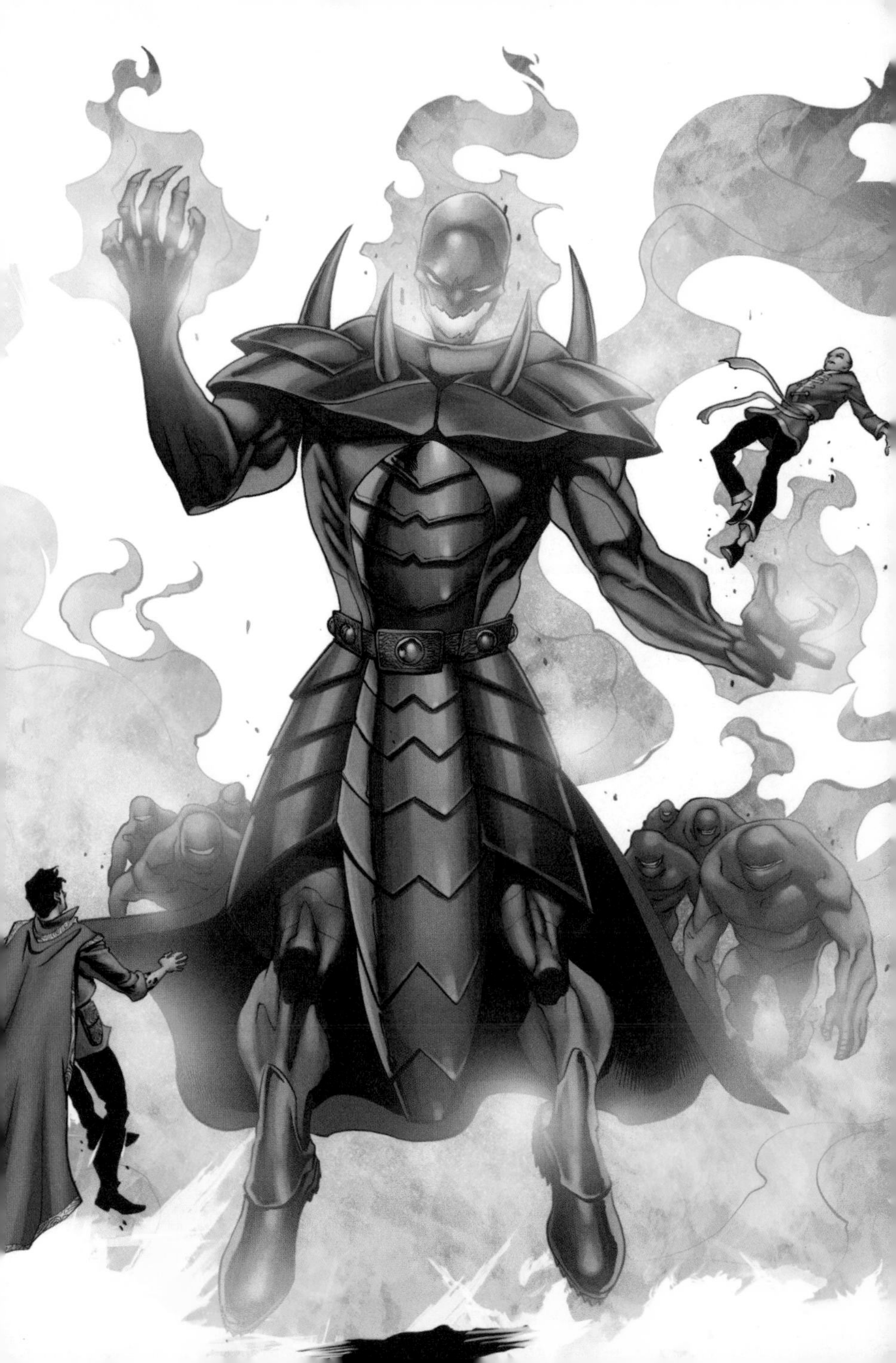

Sanctum, he needed to calm himself and learn Dormammu's master plan.

"He's right here," said Dormammu, revealing Wong's lifeless body hanging in the air beside him. **"Wong lives, but his spirit is trapped on the Astral Plane and you will never get it back!"**

Doctor Strange was boiling with anger. "And *you* were behind it all?" he asked. "The **werelizards, the vampires**, and **the demon elves—** those were all *your* doing?"

"Yes, Doctor. It was I who created the numerous magical distractions across the city. I used my power to control weaker beings that

would attack your world out of fear. I knew that attending to all of these bizarre occurrences would exhaust, frustrate, and confuse you. Then I could strike you at your weakest point."

"You're as clever and devious as ever," said Strange. "So why summon me back here? Why not simply destroy my friend and my home and be done with it?"

"Because I want you to watch me take everything you have!" said Dormammu, firing a flaming bolt of energy at Doctor Strange. "I want your Sanctum. I want your weapons. And once I get those, I will take control of the Earthly Plane," he threatened.

The heat intensified. **Dormammu** used his dark power to open a gateway to bring through an army of **Mindless Ones**, who began smashing the Sanctum to bits. The Mindless Ones were giant, silent creatures with one purpose: **TOTAL DESTRUCTION.**

Dormammu cackled as he watched them ravage everything in sight. **"I will plunge this world into darkness and rule it for all of eternity while you watch. There is no escape. It's over, Stephen Strange!"**

"QUIET!" shouted Doctor Strange. He paused for a moment, and a sly smile appeared on his face. He had sensed a shift in the magical realm.

"What are you smiling about?" growled Dormammu.

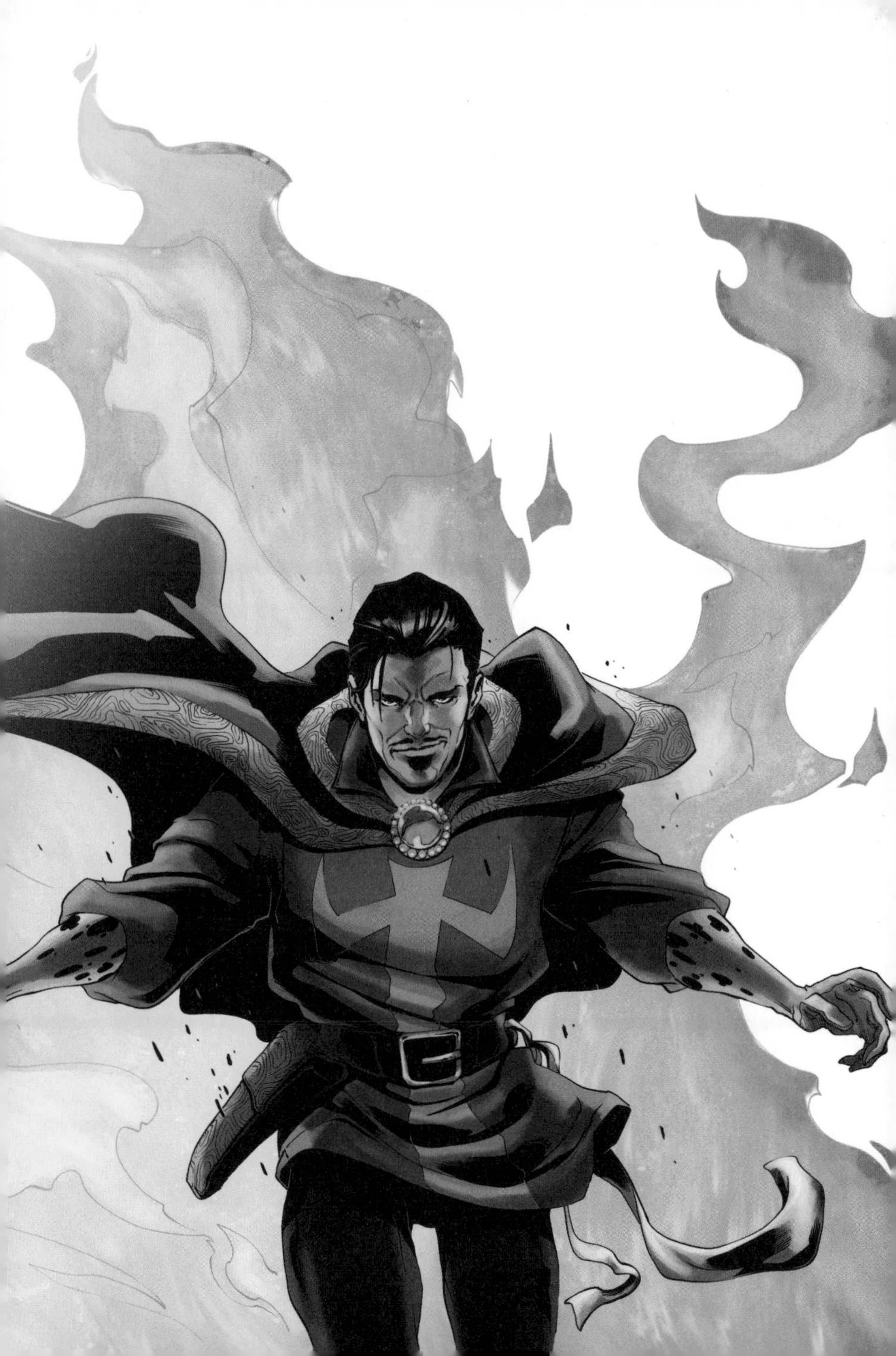

"My *friends* are here and *you're* in trouble," said Doctor Strange. A rumbling shook the Sanctum, and in a brilliant flash of light, **Scarlet Witch**, **Brother Voodoo**, **Iron Fist**, and White Tiger appeared, ready for battle. "Let us help you finish this."

"It's not over *yet*, Dormammu," said Doctor Strange. He calmly walked over to **the Ax of Angarruumus** and removed it from its perch. "Shall we dance?"

CHAPTER 10

Doctor Strange and his friends stood tall against **Dormammu** and **the Mindless Ones**. Scarlet Witch, Brother Voodoo, Iron Fist, White Tiger, and Doctor Strange were a *team*, and together they were ready to take on the lord of the Dark Dimension once and for all.

Dormammu gazed at the assembled heroes and cackled. **"Scarlet Witch? You are nothing,"** he said dismissively. Many villains had underestimated Scarlet Witch over the years.

She had defeated all of them. They believed she was delicate and sensitive, traits they viewed as weaknesses. In reality, Scarlet Witch was a powerful sorceress who used her mysterious hex bolts in a variety of ways.

She fired one at Dormammu as he recoiled in surprise. He wasn't expecting such raw, unpredictable power. She blasted him again and again in quick succession. Dormammu was *angry*. Lucky for him, he had an army of creatures at his command. **"Mindless Ones, shatter these heroes beyond repair!"**

Doctor Strange wasn't having it. He leaped into the middle of a battalion of Mindless Ones and swung **the Ax of Angarruumus** in a complete circle, knocking back the attacking beasts. For a moment it even looked as if he was enjoying himself.

Scarlet Witch took the lead, steering each hero in the right direction. "**White Tiger**, you'll need to subdue the Mindless Ones as best you can," she said. "Keep them busy and prevent them from destroying the Sanctum."

"You got it," said White Tiger, jumping into action and attuning herself to the tiger amulet's power. **"Time to take down some Mindless Ones!"** She launched herself into the air and kicked one right in the face.

Two of them charged White Tiger from either side as a third attacked from the front. A normal hero might've felt trapped, but the nimble White Tiger flipped into the air and the three Mindless Ones crashed into one another. "I love it when the bad guys do your job for you," she said, moving on to the next challenge.

"Iron Fist, grab all the weapons and relics so Dormammu can't get his hands on them," instructed Scarlet Witch.

Iron Fist was excited but also nervous. Handling a bunch of magic weapons sounded pretty

cool, but one mistake and he might accidentally open a portal to doom. He leaped across a group of attacking Mindless Ones and began swiping pieces of Doctor Strange's collection.

"This is actually kind of fun. I don't even have to use my powers," said Iron Fist as a Mindless One lumbered up behind him. It raised its giant hands, ready to smash its enemy into a million pieces, but Iron Fist's acute mystical senses alerted him to the situation. He summoned the power of **the mystical dragon Shou-Lao**, and his fist glowed bright with energy. In the blink of an eye, the young hero had turned and unleashed the full power of his Iron Fist punch on the Mindless One, knocking it down with a giant **BOOM!** "Oh well. I guess I spoke too soon. Nighty-night!" He gently stepped over the beast.

Dormammu saw his minions being defeated and decided to turn up the heat. **"Flames of the Faltine, swallow this Sanctum whole!"** he commanded, and the ceiling began to drip with fire. A loud belch shook the heroes as a pit of flames opened in the middle of the room.

"I can't access the Astral Plane. Dormammu is blocking my entry," Doctor Strange confessed.

"Let *me* handle this," said Brother Voodoo. "Doctor Strange, get ready to grab Wong."

"HA-HA-HA! You cannot be serious, Brother Voodoo." Dormammu cackled. **"I rule an entire dimension, and you are just a man wearing a necklace of skulls. Do you really think you're powerful enough to stop me?"**

"Maybe *I'm* not powerful enough to stop you," countered Voodoo, "but thankfully, I have friends like Doctor Strange. And he happened to share a special spell with me for just this sort of occasion.

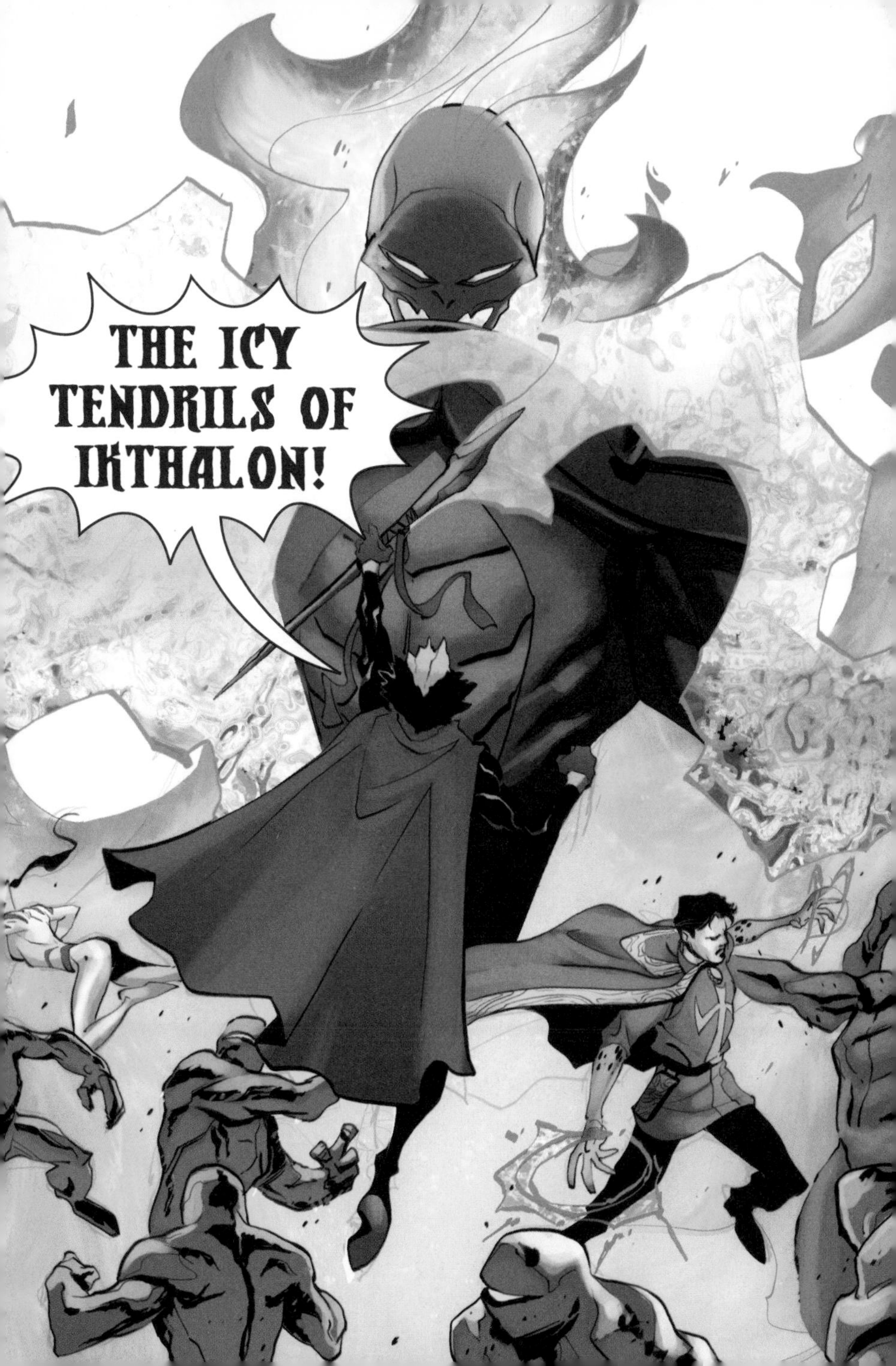
THE ICY TENDRILS OF IKTHALON!

Brother Voodoo reached toward Dormammu and fired a massive bolt of freezing energy, trapping the demon in a block of ice.

Scarlet Witch hastily ran to retrieve Wong and keep his body safe from harm. **"Now, Stephen! While Dormammu is frozen!"** she shouted.

Doctor Strange entered the Astral Plane and quickly located **Wong**. "Hello, old friend," Strange said. "It's good to see you."

"I'd like to go home now," Wong replied.

Strange used his magic to pull Wong's spirit back to the Earthly Plane, where he awoke safely in his body. Wong took a look around at all the chaos occurring within the Sanctum. "I'm going to need help cleaning this up," he joked.

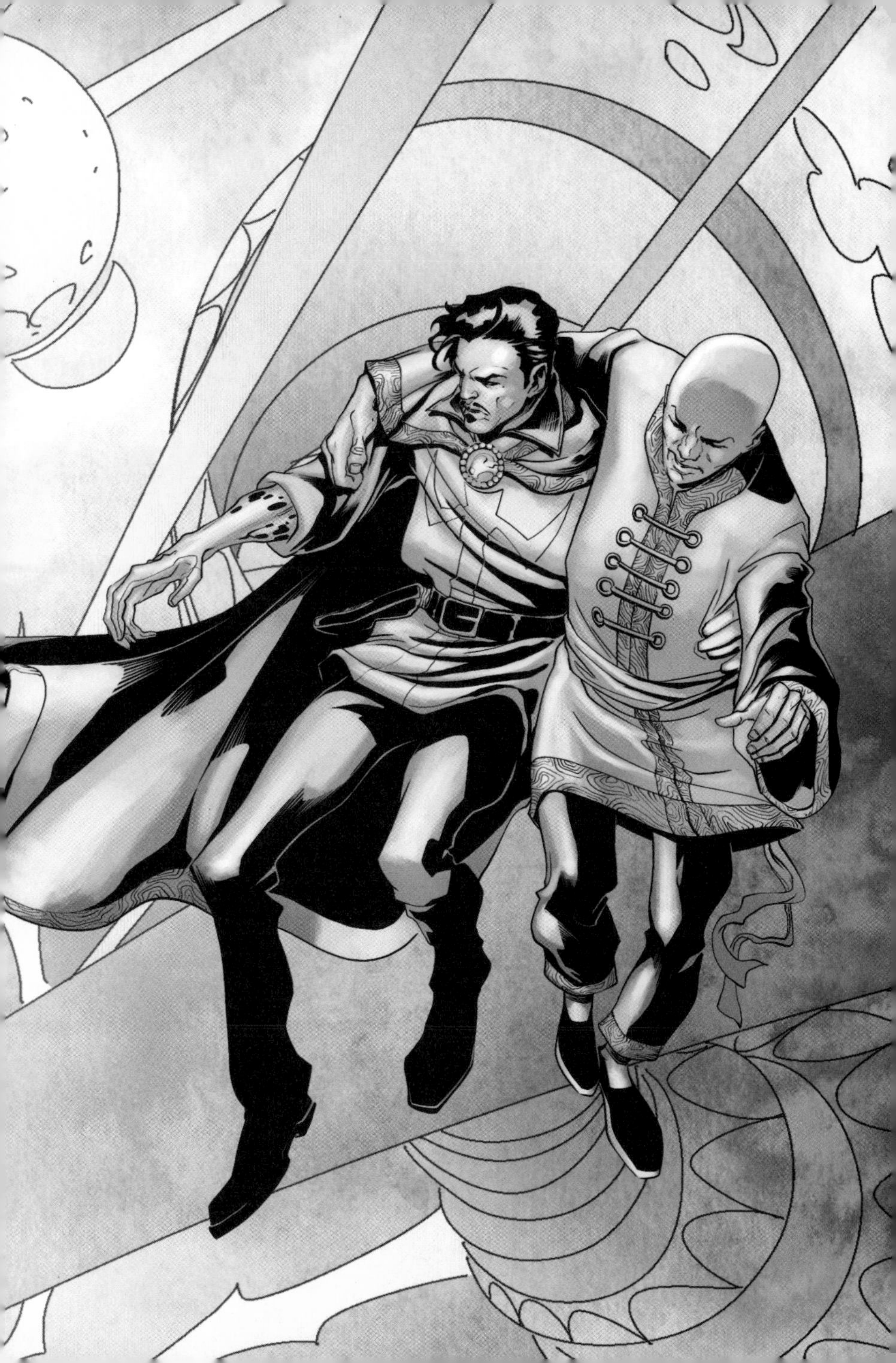

Dormammu burst free of his icy prison. He spotted Iron Fist with Doctor Strange's prized **Wand of Watoomb** and used his power to snatch it out of his hands. **"Now I will end this battle and rule the universe."**

With a smile, Iron Fist pulled another **Wand**

of Watoomb from behind his back. "Does *this* look familiar?"

"**Silly human. You know nothing of magic!**" said Dormammu. "**Prepare to meet your doom.**" In an instant the wand in his hand disappeared, leaving Dormammu confused and angry.

"I know a little *something* about magic, Dormy. Can I call you Dormy?" asked Iron Fist. "You see, a wise man once told me magic is all about *misdirection*." He handed his wand to Doctor Strange. "Would you do the honors, **Sorcerer Supreme**?"

"Gladly," said Doctor Strange, smiling.
"BY THE WAND OF WATOOMB, BEGONE FROM THIS REALM, FOUL DEMON!"

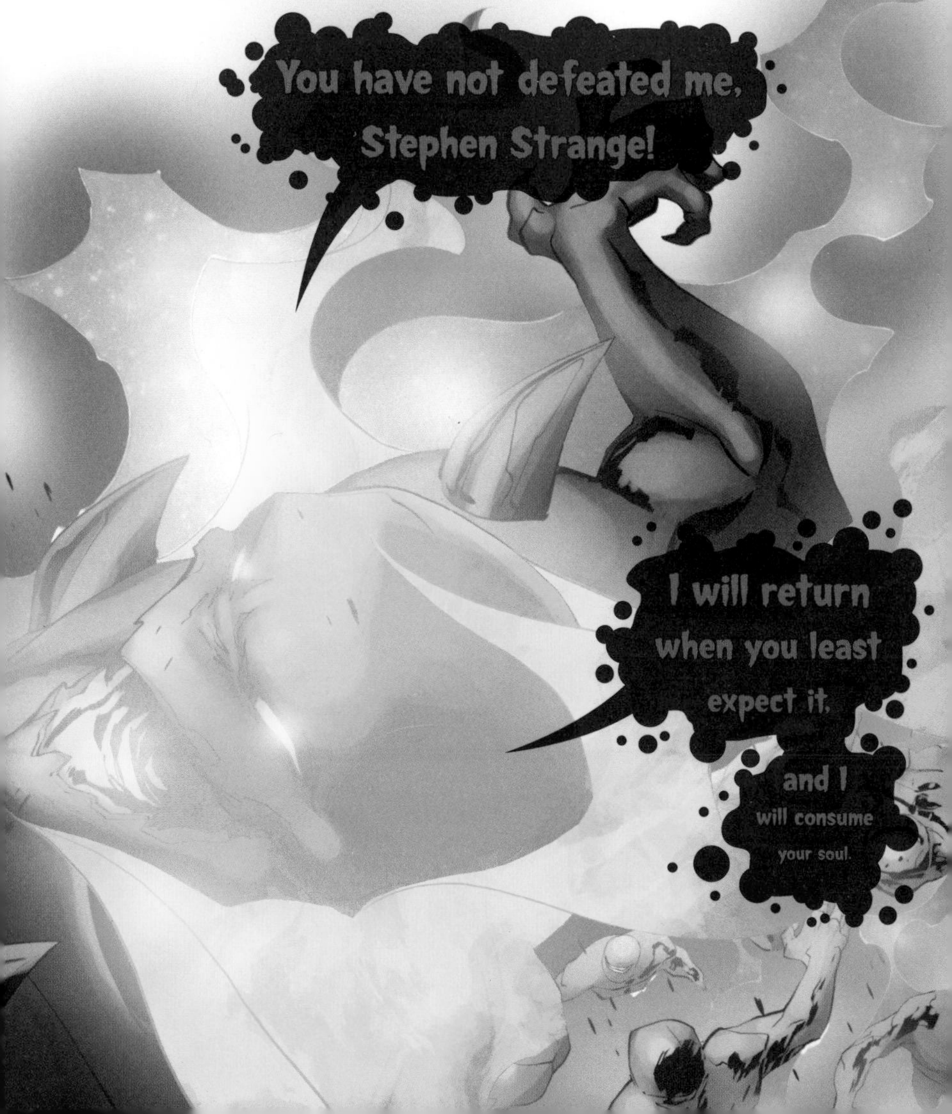
You have not defeated me, Stephen Strange!
I will return when you least expect it,
and I will consume your soul.

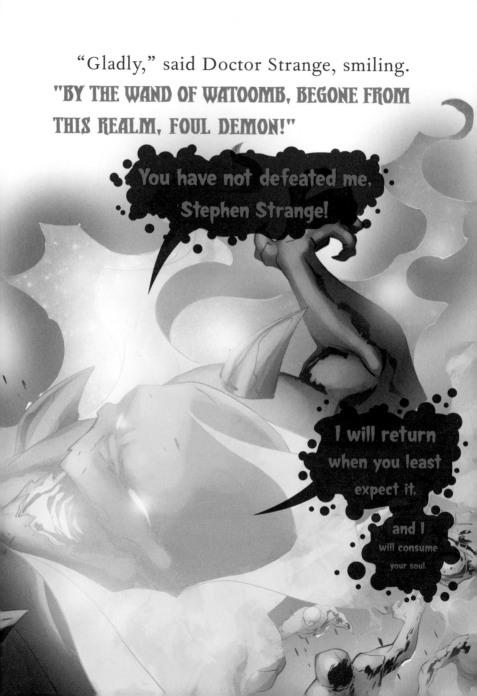

In a blaze of light, **Dormammu** and the **Mindless Ones** were gone. The battle was over, and everyone was safe at last.

Scarlet Witch smiled.

"Thanks for the illusion, Wanda. Old Dormy thought he had the real thing," said Iron Fist. "And nice wand work, Doc."

Doctor Strange glanced around the room, overwhelmed. "I cannot thank you all enough," he said. "I owe each of you a debt of gratitude."

"No, Stephen," replied Brother Voodoo. "We owe *you*. Without your advice and guidance, we might not have been able to defeat Dormammu."

A naked **soul rat** scurried across Iron Fist's feet.

"Yikes!" he cried out.

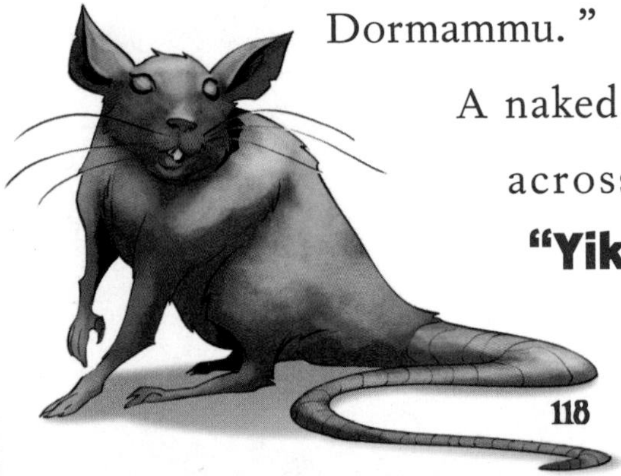

"Well, if you don't mind," said Doctor Strange, "there is a bit of cleaning to be done."

The heroes began using their powers to repair the damage. Scarlet Witch used her hex abilities to heal the burnt areas of the Sanctum. Iron Fist focused his senses, eliminating all traces of Dormammu's evil presence. Brother Voodoo blew magic dusts into the air, adding a new layer of protection to the Sanctum. White Tiger used super strength to reassemble parts of Strange's damaged home.

"Dark magic," grumbled Doctor Strange. "I imagine the scent will linger."

"I'll light a fragrant candle. It'll be gone soon enough," said Wong. "Now, more important, who wants *SOUP*?"

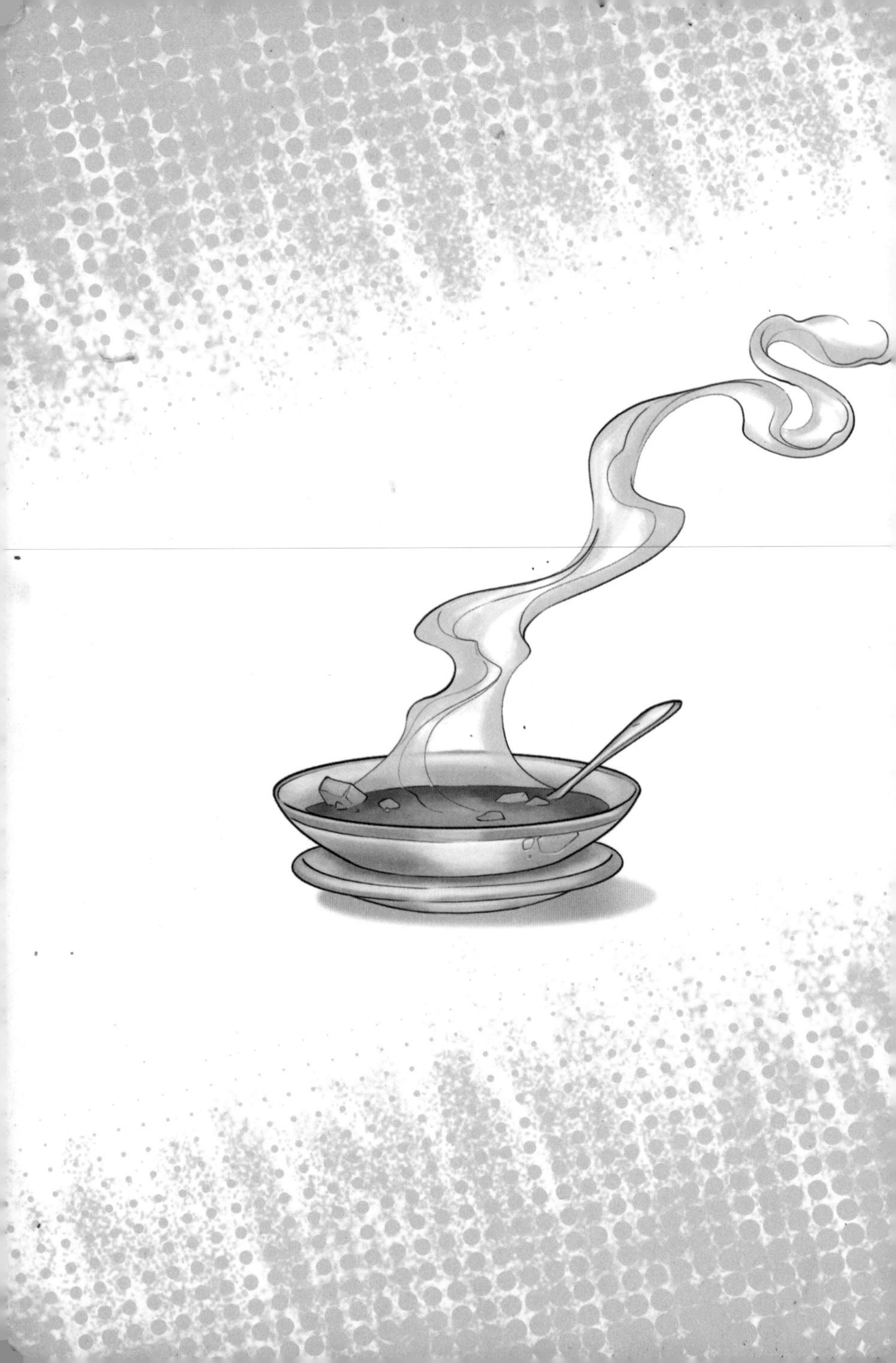